"I want you to understand what it was like for me being forced into marriage when I wasn't ready for it."

"I understand perfectly," Leah said frigidly.

"I married you under duress. I would not have married you otherwise. I was not ready to make that commitment to any woman. Better I left you alone than shared your bed...."

"Tell me, is there some point to this deeply unpleasant walk down memory lane?" Leah prompted stiffly.

Nik treated her to his wolfish smile. "I'm ready to settle down into being married."

LYNNE GRAHAM was born in Northern Ireland and has been a keen romance reader since her teens. She is very happily married, with an understanding husband, who has learned to cook since she started to write! Her three children, two of whom are adopted, keep her on her toes. She also has a very large wolfhound, who knocks over everything with her tail, and an even-more-adored mongrel, who rules everybody. When time allows, Lynne is a keen gardener and loves experimenting with Italian cookery.

Books by Lynne Graham

HARLEQUIN PRESENTS
1551—TEMPESTUOUS REUNION
1696—A VENGEFUL PASSION
1712—ANGEL OF DARKNESS
1758—BOND OF HATRED

Don't miss any of our special offers. Write to us at the following address for information on our newest releases.

Harlequin Reader Service
U.S.: 3010 Walden Ave., P.O. Box 1325, Buffalo, NY 14269
Canadian: P.O. Box 609, Fort Erie, Ont. L2A 5X3

LYNNE GRAHAM

The Unfaithful Wife

Harlequin Books

TORONTO • NEW YORK • LONDON
AMSTERDAM • PARIS • SYDNEY • HAMBURG
STOCKHOLM • ATHENS • TOKYO • MILAN
MADRID • WARSAW • BUDAPEST • AUCKLAND

ISBN 0-373-11779-5

THE UNFAITHFUL WIFE

First North American Publication 1995.

Copyright © 1995 by Lynne Graham.

This edition published by arrangement with Harlequin Books S.A.

® and TM are trademarks of the publisher. Trademarks indicated with
® are registered in the United States Patent and Trademark Office, the
Canadian Trade Marks Office and in other countries.

Printed in U.S.A.

CHAPTER ONE

WITH a fleeting glance over her shoulder, Leah hurried down the steps and into the wine bar. It was dark and crowded with lunchtime drinkers. She couldn't see Paul. She wasn't tall enough to see past the clumps of business-suited men standing around. A nervous tremor shot through her as she burrowed through the male clusters. She was so terrified of being seen, recognised. It was a relief to espy Paul's golden head in a far corner.

He stood up as she approached, tall, sophisticated and very attractive, and her heart swelled with pride. 'You're late,' he complained.

'Sorry, I couldn't get away.' Short of breath, Leah dropped down on to a seat and couldn't help spinning another glance around in fearful search of a familiar face.

'Stop that. You're on the wrong side of town to be seen.'

Leah bent her silver-blonde head, her face flushed and taut. 'That man in the corner is staring at me!'

'Most men stare at beautiful women . . . and you are exquisitely beautiful, my love,' Paul murmured in a low, intimate tone, reaching for her slender-boned hand. 'It gives me a real kick watching every male head turn when you walk by.'

'Does it?' Still unaccustomed to his compliments, Leah looked up at him with a shy uncertainty that was oddly at variance with her designer suit. Her flawless face between the wings of her sleekly swept up silver-blonde hair was rapt, her sapphire-blue eyes bright as the jewels in her ears.

'Why don't we go back to my apartment?' Paul ran a finger along her full lower lip and smiled smoothly as her skin heated.

Leah stiffened. 'I can't...not yet; you know how I feel,' she muttered in a stifled voice. Fear sprung up inside her as his handsome face turned hard and cold.

'And you know how I feel, Mrs Andreakis. Bloody frustrated, if you must know!'

Leah went white. 'Paul, please...'

'For all I know, you're just playing a little game with me while your husband's out of town.'

Pain and distress filled her eyes. 'I love you...'

'Then when are you going to tell him you want a divorce?' Paul demanded.

If possible, Leah went even paler, a hunted look tightening her exquisite features. 'Soon... I just have to pick the right moment.'

'Considering that on average he only sleeps one night a month under the same roof as you, I could still be sitting here this time next year. Maybe you're in love with the bastard——'

'How could I be?' She bent her head, her hands clenching tightly together. 'You know we don't have a normal marriage.'

'And wouldn't the tabloids just love to get a load of that!' Paul sniggered.

'I don't think that's funny, Paul.'

'Well, the only thing that keeps me going is the knowledge that I may not be your lover, but he isn't either. And you've got to admit that that's a real mystery. Look at you,' Paul mused. 'The virgin bride five years down the road and yet he's rarely seen in public without some beautiful bimbo clinging to his arm. Maybe he's a closet gay.'

Her sensitive stomach curdled. She must have been mad to tell Paul the truth about her marriage. Not, of course, that he would do anything with it. She trusted him absolutely but she was aware that she had been dangerously indiscreet in her need to soothe his jealousy of Nik. *Nik*... The very blood in her veins went cold when she faced up to what she still had ahead of her.

'Don't talk about him like that,' she urged tightly.

'You think the table is bugged? You're scared stiff of him, aren't you? I don't think you're ever going to pick up the courage to tell him you want your freedom. I think I'm wasting my time——'

'No... no, never,' Leah whispered frantically, the thought of losing him filling her with panic. She just couldn't go back to what her life had been for the past five years. Empty, without focus, boring. Before Paul, every day had stretched endlessly in front of her. She didn't have a social life. She didn't have friends. She was watched everywhere she went. The door of her prison had slammed shut on her wedding-day and she had been so dumb, so naïve, she hadn't even realised it until she'd tried to move beyond the bars.

'Then when?' he pressed moodily.

'Soon... I promise you.'

'I don't see why you can't just move out bag and baggage. It's not as though you don't have all the evidence you need to divorce him. Adultery is not about to go out of fashion with Nik Andreakis around.'

'I have to do it right, Paul. Don't you see that I owe him that?'

'I don't see that you owe him anything. In the eyes of the Church and the law, he's not even your husband,' Paul persisted impressively.

Leah glanced at her watch and uttered a gasp of dismay. 'I have to go!'

Paul caught her by the shoulders and kissed her with practised expertise. 'I'll phone,' he promised. 'Love you, darling.'

Leah fled. It was three blocks to the fashionable hair-dressers where she had been booked in for a long session of massage and beauty treatment. She took terrible risks to meet up with Paul and her head told her that the longer she put off asking Nik for a divorce, the more chance there was of her being found out. But, then, what would it really matter?

Nik didn't care what she did. She saw him maybe once a month when he stopped over in London, sometimes not even that over the past year. He might request that she play hostess for a business dinner, but of late even those requests had been few and far between. If he had to communicate with her, he did so through his staff.

In their entire marriage, Nik had never once taken her out in public. Not for dinner, not to the theatre, not to a party. Nik pursued his glittering social life with other women on his arm...never, ever his wife. He slept in his own wing of the house...and even that handful of nights a year that he stayed under the same roof she had heard him go out late and return after dawn, so those nights didn't really count either.

For an instant, as she flew through the side-entrance of the hairdressers, she remembered when she had lain awake crying and listening for him, wondering in despair what was wrong with her, what she had done, what she had not done, what she could possibly do to make him notice her and acknowledge her existence. Angrily she thrust the memory away. Time had taken care of that kind of nonsense. The child bride had grown up and wised up.

'I'm so sorry. I forgot my appointment,' Leah murmured at the reception desk and as usual she insisted on paying anyway and she tipped as if there were no tomorrow. The proprietor, Charlie, came up to her and offered to fit her in immediately but she sighed and said she was running late and sat down to wait for her chauffeur to draw up outside.

'Oh, by the way, Mrs Andreakis——' Charlie lowered his head, his beaded locks swinging colourfully '—your bodyguard called in with a message for you.'

Leah went rigid, turned white as a ghost.

'Relax.' Wry brown eyes met hers. 'I said you were in the massage-room.'

Leah turned scarlet. 'Thank you,' she managed jerkily.

'I'd better give you the message,' he whispered. 'Mr Andreakis is waiting for you at home.'

Nik was what? Nik was waiting for her... Nik who had never waited for her once in five years? Nik was home when he wasn't due back in London for another fortnight? Involuntarily, Leah shivered, her stomach turning over sickly. For a split-second she was consumed by the sort of panic that made people jump out windows in a fire. Sheer cold terror.

Charlie settled down beside her, his hands planted on his knees. 'Baby, you're not cut out for this game you're playing——'

'I don't know what you're——'

'You've been coming here every week for five years. And the last couple of months what you've been feeling has been just blazing all over your face.' He sighed. 'But I don't want to go down in history as the idiot stupid enough to give Nik Andreakis's wife an alibi. He's the kind of guy who probably breaks fingers. I get the shakes just thinking about it.'

Shame washed over her. 'I'm sorry.'

'And I'm sorry I can't be more help because it's been kinda nice seeing you happy for a change.'

'Mrs Andreakis ... ?'

Leah flinched as her bodyguard, Boyce, cast a big, dark shadow over her. As she stood, he cast a suspicious, cold look at Charlie, who had been too physically close to his employer's wife for his liking.

As soon as the door slammed on the limousine, her composure collapsed. Charlie knew she was seeing someone. Dear God, she felt so humiliated. She also felt guilty as hell. Her hairdresser was afraid of being dragged into a marital furore. Not that there was the slightest chance of that happening when Nik couldn't give two hoots what she did. But cheerful, wisecracking Charlie, who had laughed her out of many a depression over the years, had been genuinely scared.

Everyone was afraid of Nik. And yet she had never heard him shout. Early on in their marriage Leah had walked in mortal terror of him until it had slowly sunk in on her, with the drip effect of his icy indifference, that she barely existed as a human being on his scale of importance. He had married her to gain the shares her father had signed over to her. She had been part of a business deal, nothing more.

And yet there had been times at the beginning when she could have sworn that Nik looked at her with veiled loathing, when his voice could say the lightest things and sound like a whiplash of naked threat, when his very presence in the same room had made her feel menaced . . . and that was when she had learnt to hug the background, never draw attention to herself, avoid him whenever possible. She had assumed that he resented having had to marry her to get the shares. Yet divorce had always been within his reach. It was a mystery Leah had yet to fathom out.

And now Nik, who had not varied his schedule in five long, endless years, had come home unexpectedly. That fact returned to haunt her, anxious though she had been to evade it. Her fingers clenched white-knuckled around her bag as she climbed the steps of the vast Georgian terraced house. The unfaithful wife, she thought painfully.

But she wasn't his wife, not his *real* wife, she reminded herself, just as she had often done in the weeks since she had met Paul. She should have demanded her freedom a long time ago. But her father would have been outraged and bitterly disappointed.

Leah had spent the first seventeen years of her life pleasing her father, Max, in every way she could. She had done as he advised five years ago. She had married Nik and it had been the biggest mistake of her life. Nik had taken her freedom and given nothing in return. But that time was past, she reminded herself. It was almost two months since her father had died, the heart condition which had endangered his health for years having finally taken its toll.

'Mr Andreakis is waiting for you in the drawing-room,' Petros the butler informed her.

Leah hovered, nervous tension biting. As a rule, she didn't see Nik until he sat down at the dinner-table. The belief that something was wrong attacked her again.

He was standing by the marble fireplace, six feet two inches of overwhelmingly masculine male. Once she had looked at him and her heart had sung, her knees had weakened and her voice had caught in her throat. Now Leah saw him always as if through a glass wall. Learning to detach herself had been lesson one.

Nik Andreakis, the legendary Greek tycoon, possessor of fabled wealth and immense power. From his hand-stitched leather shoes to his fabulously tailored mohair- and silk-blend pearl-grey suit, he was effortlessly elegant, supremely sophisticated. A man to die for, she had thought at seventeen, her impressionable little teeny-bopper heart ready to burst with sheer excitement.

And Nik was a devastatingly handsome male animal, quite stunningly gorgeous by any standards. Thick ebony hair, golden skin, riveting black eyes as dark as night. Wherever he went he was the focus of female attention. And he knew it, was amused by it...used it when it suited him. Once, though she rarely allowed herself to recall it, Nik had focused that elemental aura of sexual energy on her.

Something had changed...something was different. Tension thrummed in the air. Deep-set dark eyes scanned her. 'Your lipstick's smudged.'

Her fingers flew up to her mouth in a gesture of dismay. 'Is it?'

Winged ebony brows drew together in slight frown. Nik studied her intently. 'We haven't got much time, so I'll just move to the baseline. We're flying to Paris.'

Frozen with astonishment, Leah echoed, '*Paris*?'

Nik had already opened the door. 'Come on,' he said with unhidden impatience.

'You want me to go to Paris *with* you?' Leah stressed helplessly. 'Now...like right now?'

'Yes.'

'But why?'

'A little business tied up with your father's estate.' Hooded dark eyes probed the amazement that flashed across her face.

And Leah was amazed—amazed that there could be anything *left* to sort out concerning her father's estate. Although Nik had not even bothered to attend Max's funeral, he had arrogantly assumed responsibility for instructing his lawyers to deal with her father's property and possessions. While Leah had been grieving, too bound up in her loss to consider the practicalities of death, everything her father owned had been sold— *everything*!

His beautiful house, his business investments, his very furniture and personal effects had all been liquidated into cash at Nik's instruction. Leah had not been left with a single memento. Her father, Max Harrington, might never have existed for nothing remained to testify to his sixty-odd years on this earth. Leah had been appalled by Nik's insensitivity but by the time she found out it had been too late for her to intervene. The deed had been done. As usual, Nik's orders had been carried out with speedy efficiency by his obedient staff.

A quiver of helpless antagonism ran through her. She lifted her silver head high. 'Something you actually overlooked?'

'No. Something I was looking for has finally been located.' Harsh emphasis accompanied the assurance. An almost savage tension was briefly stamped in his hard, strong features as he read her mystified expression. 'At least I think it has been. For your own sake, pray that I am right,' he completed tautly.

Paling, Leah stepped back from him, the chill, the sense of threat running along her every nerve-ending. 'For *my* sake? I don't know what you're talking about.'

'I hope not.' He swung on his heel.

Leah made for the stairs. A hard hand stayed her. 'Where do you think you're going?'

'To get changed.' Sudden fear licked at her. She stared in shock at the lean, powerful hand clamped to her slender forearm. Nik never touched her...never, not even in the most passing, casual gesture.

'There's no time for that. The jet's ready for take-off.'

'Will we be coming back tonight?' Her voice rose an octave as he literally thrust her out of the house. 'I have nothing packed!'

'You'll manage.'

'What's going on?' Leah demanded frantically as the limousine drew away from the kerb.

Ignoring her with supreme disdain, Nik picked up the phone and proceeded to talk at length in Greek.

She didn't understand a word. A fleeting recollection stirred. On their wedding-day she had told him she intended to learn his language. 'Don't waste your time,' he had derided, and that had been the very first crack that appeared in her fantasy world. Before the day was at an end, the crack had widened into a yawning gulf but it had taken a lot longer for reality to banish that fantasy world she had wanted so badly.

Her temples throbbed with the tension in the air. But her inner turmoil did not show. She sat still, apparently composed, her manicured hands loosely resting on her lap. In Nik's presence she had learnt to conceal her emotions. Only that did not still the stormy flood of her hidden consternation and incomprehension.

'What is this all about?' Leah asked a second time. Silence.

Doggedly she persisted. 'I understood that Dad's estate was all settled.'

'Did you really? I wonder,' Nik responded murderously quietly.

Something in his intonation disturbed her. Her delicate profile turned. She encountered eyes as treacherous as black ice. Her stomach muscles clenched, her skin chilling. She had a sense of impending disaster so powerful that she felt briefly sick.

'If you would just explain what——?' she began.

'Why should I explain myself to you?' It was so clearly a growl of lancing derision that she was silenced.

'Young as you are, you are every man's secret fantasy...' Who would ever believe that those seductive words had been uttered by the husband who had ignored her very existence for five solid years? Yet Nik had said those words the first day they met. Why had he lied? Why had he pretended? Had he wanted those shares in that shipping line that badly? He must have done. It was patently obvious that she had never been Nik Andreakis's secret fantasy. Bitterness tremored through her. Nik had used her without conscience... as had her father, who had gloried in Nik's wealth and status.

Pained by the acknowledgement, Leah looked blankly out of the window. She longed for Paul—Paul, who hadn't even known who she was when he'd first approached her, Paul, the very first man in her life to respond to her as an individual with feelings and needs and opinions of her own. He wanted only her. He wanted her for herself. He wasn't trying to use her.

In Paris, she would tell Nik that she wanted a divorce. There would be no more procrastination. She would not risk losing Paul. And she was hungry to live a life of her own, hungry for the freedom which beckoned so tantalisingly on the horizon. Nik had stolen her youth, the teenage years when she should have been dating and having fun and *loving*. Why shouldn't she be greedy for what she had never had?

On the private jet she flicked through magazines but her mouth curled several times as she watched the stewardess hover round Nik like some harem concubine, desperate to attract the sultan's favour. The beautiful brunette had a bad dose of infatuation. Who better than Leah to recognise the symptoms? After all, she had once been a victim herself. But now she was utterly detached from Nik and prided herself on the fact.

Nik Andreakis, with his smouldering Greek temperament and movie-star looks, didn't touch her on any physical or emotional level. He was volatile, ruthless and unpredictable. The cloak of civilisation was thin. He was also manipulative, arrogant and vicious towards those who opposed or antagonised him. If she had been his *real* wife, she wouldn't have dared to sneak around with another man behind his back...

A limousine collected them at Charles de Gaulle Airport, carrying them through the heavy late afternoon traffic. The car drew up on a busy, crowded street. Leah climbed out, too proud to ask yet again where they were going but looking around. Nik strode ahead of her into the nearest building. He was carrying an executive case. And the building was a bank, she registered.

Three men were waiting in the foyer. One of them, whom she recognised as her father's solicitor, attempted to speak to her. But Nik cut him off very rudely. From below her lashes she stole a glance at her husband. Dear

God, but he was ignorant. In the wrong mood—too frequently the only mood in which Leah saw him—his manners were atrocious towards those unfortunates he considered to be lesser beings. As one of them, Leah felt a creature sympathy for the middle-aged man with his flushed, strained face.

A lift took them down to the vaults. The magical mystery tour, she reflected grimly. Were there more shares in that precious shipping line on offer? How could any man with Nik's fabulous wealth and assets be so disgustingly greedy? He had married her out of greed, hadn't he? Something for nothing. The shares had come free as her dowry.

The solicitor stuffed a key in her hand abruptly and then turned away.

''Give it to me,' Nik grated in a driven undertone, his simmering tension leaping out at her in an electrifying wave.

The key for a safety-deposit box, presumably belonging to her father, for why else would it have been put in her hand? She ignored him. For the very first time in their marriage she ignored her husband, moving forward to watch the bank executive produce the box and leave it on the table before quietly leaving the small, bare room.

'Leah...' Nik growled.

She refused to look at him. 'If it's my father's, it's mine...'

'Be very careful of what you claim.'

His savage warning pierced cold to the very centre of her body. She looked at him and was paralysed. Naked violence and aggression were etched in his ferociously taut features. She blenched, and cast the key on the table by the box in sudden surrender.

'If it's in here you can relax,' Nik murmured between clenched white teeth. 'If it isn't, you'll be lucky to see the dawn break tomorrow.'

If *what* was in there? Perspiration broke on her short upper lip. Her legs suddenly felt weak and wobbly. Her sapphire-blue eyes clung to him in sick disbelief. But he wasn't looking at her. He was inserting the key in the box with a hand that wasn't quite steady.

She licked her dry lips. There was something more than shares at stake, something terrible enough to make even Nik Andreakis threaten to come apart at the seams... She had never seen him close to the edge, never dreamt that he could lose control, but she was seeing it now.

The box was full of papers. With a burst of guttural Greek, Nik began to rifle through them, discarding letters and photos which spilled in careless disarray across the table. He was pale and taut, his evident search becoming visibly more agitated.

Leah focused on an envelope addressed to someone she had never heard of. She didn't even recognise the writing. And then she glimpsed a large, glossy photograph. In stark colour, it depicted a number of men and women engaged in... In shock and disgust, Leah averted her eyes again. She started to tremble. Why had her father kept such an obscene thing in his possession?

'What is this stuff?' she whispered, since it was blatantly obvious that Nik knew far more about the contents of that box than she did. He had flicked past that photo without an ounce of reaction or surprise.

'What is it?' An edged laugh fell from his compressed mouth but there was no humour in the sound. 'It's a box of broken lives! Other people's secrets. Your father lived off his victims and their fear like some filthy cockroach!'

White as a sheet, Leah gaped at him. 'How dare you talk about my father like that?'

Nik wasn't listening to her. He was still feverishly sorting through the papers. 'That he should leave me to clear up this filth is the final insult. I, Nik Andreakis, reduced to soiling my hands because I cannot trust any other person alive with this obscene collection of human errors! *His* trophies! He kept them to the last instead of destroying them! *Cristo* . . . the evil old bastard . . .'

Only the cold wall was supporting Leah. She could not credit the crime that her late father was being accused of. Her mind was a complete blank over a seething sea of sick turmoil. 'What are you saying?' Her voice was so weak it was a thread of sound.

'Are you deaf?' Nik slung her a savage look of unconcealed loathing. 'Why do you think I married you? For your chocolate-box looks and your convent education?' he sneered. 'For your ability to act like a lady and fix stupid flower arrangements all over my house?'

'The shares,' she mumbled, shaking all over.

'There were no shares!' he raked back at her, the volume of his voice echoing off the walls with a rage that made her quail helplessly. 'There were *never* any shares. That shipping line didn't even exist!'

'You're lying,' Leah framed through bloodless lips, barely able to stay upright.

Nik's attention was on the document he held in his hand. Suddenly, without any warning, he smashed his clenched fist down brutally hard on the tabletop. '*Theos mou* . . .' he intoned with vicious bite. 'It's only a copy!'

'A c-copy of what?' As the table jumped, Leah flinched, plastering herself back against the wall, sick and dizzy.

'And this is the end of the trail . . .'

Nik prowled towards her like a tiger about to spring for her throat and drag her down. 'He gave the original to you, didn't he?' he murmured with lethal quietness, glittering black eyes settling on her with violent force. 'He gave it to you to keep safe . . .'

'G-gave what to me?' Leah was so distraught she could barely articulate. She couldn't think either.

'You know what I'm talking about. Not so innocent after all, it seems,' he breathed, backing her into a corner. 'If it isn't here, you have it. Max was no fool. He knew I'd dump you like a hot potato if I got my hands on it. So he gave it to you... so where is it?'

'*Stop it*!' Leah gasped strickenly, fearfully. 'Leave me alone!'

'If you don't tell me where that certificate is... you're in more danger now than you have ever been in your life,' Nik spelt out, waves of raw aggression splintering from his lowering stance a mere foot from her. 'I have lived with blackmail for five years to protect my family. I will not live with it *one* day longer!'

He had said the word, that terrifying word, and it danced about on the edges of the living nightmare she was being forced to endure. 'Blackmail'... It wasn't true, couldn't be true. Her father could not have been a blackmailer. On the edge of collapse, Leah fought to stand her ground.

'I always wondered whether he intended it this way... that you should be my life sentence,' Nik vented in a seething undertone. 'But I tell you now, *pethi mou*, I would sooner go to prison for putting my hands round that scrawny little throat and strangling the life force from your body. *That* would be the only life sentence I could live with!'

Terrified beyond endurance, Leah watched his dark, threatening face above hers black out and finally, mercifully vanish as she slid down the wall in a dead faint.

CHAPTER TWO

LEAH recovered consciousness in the limousine. Nik was bending over her just as he had been doing before she'd passed out. In one frantic movement she jackknifed back from him and plastered herself up against the far door while she fumbled madly for the release mechanism, uncaring that they were in the midst of fast-moving traffic. 'Get away from me!' she screeched in panic.

'Fragile little creature, aren't you? A bundle of rampant nerves all of a sudden.' Lounging back in a disturbing attitude of fluid relaxation, Nik surveyed her with unashamed satisfaction and a sardonic smile, his aggression cloaked, his temper back under control. 'So where is that certificate?'

Her fingernails clenched painfully into her palms, etching purple crescents on the tender flesh. She needed that pain to be assured that Nik was still talking in the same nightmare fashion that he had been employing inside that suffocating little room. 'I've already told you that I don't know what you're talking about.'

'Well, if you didn't know you know now and I want an answer.'

'I can't believe my father was a blackmailer——'

'Dirty, isn't it?' Nik treated her to a scrutiny empty of even the tiniest vein of compassion. 'But then he was a professional of the very highest quality. His field was the rich and famous and the skeletons he dug out of closets had to be really juicy ones. He was very good at what he did,' Nik drawled impassively. 'He never milked his victims totally dry. He never drove anyone to the brink of trying to kill him. He made them pay for so

20

long and then he let them off the hook but he kept the
evidence of their misdeeds to protect himself. He made
a fortune...'

'I won't believe it!' Leah slung back shakily. 'I won't
believe any of this!'

'Do you think he kept pornographic pictures in that
box just for fun?'

Leah's stomach curdled. She lowered her pounding
head.

'Now if he took the trouble to retain a copy of the
juicy skeleton he trailed out of *my* family closet——'
Nik's deep voice held a renewed edge of harshness
'—he also kept the original of the certificate, and since
I have exhausted every other avenue it is obvious to me
that he must have given it to you.'

'He didn't give anything to me!' There was a quiver
of hysteria in her tremulous response. She was in shock—
deep shock—and in no state to combat his continuing
pressure for her to produce something that she had not
even known existed and certainly didn't have.

'You can't hold it over me. Just try and I will break
you...'

'You're crazy!' she suddenly sobbed.

'This far, I have been remarkably kind and patient. I
have been on a leash for five years,' Nik grated in an
embittered undertone. 'I was only safe as long as I stayed
married to you. I thought you might run home to Daddy.
But you never did and one thing did become clear to
me, gruesomely clear over the years. You are in love with
me——'

'What?' Leah interrupted shakily.

'You are obsessed with me. Do you think I don't know
this?' Nik sent her a shimmering look of contempt. 'Any
normal woman would have left me by now and given
up all hope of having her love returned... but not you!
You stayed the course, loyal to the bitter end, obscenely

faithful and well-behaved, giving me no excuse to complain of the devil's bargain I made!'

'Faithful'? Hysteria was tearing at her convulsing throat. Dear heaven, he actually believed what he was saying! Nik believed that she loved him. He thought she had stayed because she loved him. Paul's name hovered on the very tip of her tongue but sixth sense warned her not to muddy the waters further. One thing at a time...only which? she wondered wildly. Life as she knew it had been shattered in the space of a few hours.

'I am not in love with you,' she murmured with as much dignity as she could contrive, her teeth gritting behind her peach-tinted lips. Absolute humiliation engulfed her as she appreciated that all along Nik had been thinking that his neglected, unwanted wife was just dying of love for him in spite of his complete indifference towards her. The ego he must have...the utter, unashamed conceit.

'Listen, you're talking to the guy who was your seventeenth birthday present!' he slung back with savage derision.

'I b-beg your pardon?'

'Did you pick me out of some society magazine? Or did you see me in the flesh first? Did you take one look and rush to Daddy and say, "Daddy, this is the one I want!"?'

He was serious. He was actually serious. Her lower lip had parted company from the upper, a hectic pink firing her cheeks to dispel her previous pallor. 'You have to be out of your mind!'

'We are going to have this conversation. I have waited five years to stage it!' Nik asserted, skimming her with glittering dark eyes. 'All I know is that dear Max did your dirty work for you. I was hunted down like an animal——'

'You are an animal...an insult to the species!' Leah abruptly burst out. 'And your conceit is staggering!'

'*Cristo* . . . my perfect lady of a wife can actually raise her voice,' Nik drawled, surveying her with flaring dark eyes. 'You don't like the truth. It hurts your pride. But I know I was trapped quite deliberately. I didn't even know who your father was that first time I came to the house. I was lured there by a third party, offering me a business proposition. And your father just so happened not to be available when I arrived.

'But, lo and behold, you were. Romantically tending flowers in the conservatory, wearing something understated and white, literally armed to the teeth with virginal wiles . . . *Theos*, I remember it so well.'

'It wasn't like that!' she gasped in outrage.

'Any hot-blooded Greek would have looked twice and lingered,' Nik told her with scorn. 'And there you were, all shy smiles and blushes, eating me up with those big blue eyes as if you hadn't had a square meal in a week!'

'*Stop it*!' Leah hissed, her voice breaking.

Nik studied her with unyielding derision, his beautiful mouth twisting. 'So I was invited to dinner and you played the piano like a concert pianist and sang like an angel. Your every cultured virtue was paraded for my philistine benefit and somehow business never came into it. It might interest you to know, *pethi mou*, that I only had two questions I wanted answered that night but couldn't ask——'

'Really?' Leah was staring blankly into space, every ounce of her remaining self-discipline directed at rescuing her shattered composure and combating the painful tidal wave of memories threatening to assail her. Two very different people . . . one encounter . . . such differing recollections of the same event.

'Were you over the age of consent? And did Daddy intend to protect you from the big bad world out there and sexual predators like me? Marriage was not, nor would it ever have been, on my mind.'

Nausea stirred inside her, and a bitter tide of mortification she could not withstand followed in its wake.

'Whose idea was it that I stay to dinner?'

Leah froze.

'I thought so,' Nik breathed. 'Your idea. You told him you wanted me and that was that. He went digging and he dug up something that only two people alive knew about and neither of them would ever have talked about it!'

'What did he dig up?' she heard herself whisper helplessly.

'You *know* . . . Max had plenty of warning that he was on borrowed time. He didn't go to his grave without passing that secret on to you,' Nik asserted softly.

'He passed nothing on to me . . .'

'And if you don't have it you have to know who *has*.'

The chauffeur opened the door beside her and she almost fell out into the fresh air. She gazed down the quiet residential street in near panic. She wanted to run. She knew where she was: Nik's Paris apartment where she had spent a quite unforgettable wedding night alone. He was unleashing everything on her at once, drowning her in a sea of shattering revelations, grinding her down with confusion, pain and humiliation.

'Try it,' Nik said very quietly. 'Run and see what happens. I wouldn't let you get as far as the street corner.'

Trembling, ashen, Leah entered the foyer in front of him and stepped into the lift.

'Memories . . .' Nik taunted, with a barbaric smile, as if he could see inside her.

Leah knew she was still in shock. She said nothing, knew she wasn't up to the challenge. Nik had been prepared. Nik had been waiting for this day, craving its arrival, longing for his revenge . . . just as he must have longed for her father's death to set him free from her.

'There are many functions I can perform to order but sharing a bed with you sadly wasn't one of them,' he delivered. 'He could make me marry you but he couldn't follow me into the bedroom and force me to——'

'*Shut up!*' she screamed at him, the hysterical demand reverberating around the steel walls of the lift.

'So why did you never tell him that?' Nik persisted, going for the jugular when she was at her lowest ebb with predictable calculation. 'Why didn't you ever tell him the truth about our marriage? Don't tell me that Max wasn't desperate to hear the patter of tiny feet which would have made your position more secure!'

Her hands flew up to cover her convulsing face, a stinging flood of moisture dammed up behind her eyelids. 'Please...no more,' she whispered, and she didn't care that she was begging.

A pair of hands gripped her narrow shoulders. '*Ne*...yes, you kept quiet about your pitifully empty marital bed all these years. Why?'

With a sudden superhuman effort which took him by surprise, Leah tore herself free and fled across the hall of the huge penthouse apartment and down the bedroom corridor. She picked a room at the very end and vanished into the *en suite* bolting the door behind her. Slowly she slid down the back of the door and then she was forced to fly up again and cope with the shuddering spasms of sickness tearing at her abdomen. When it was over, she took off her clothes with the attitude of a sleepwalker and entered the shower cubicle.

My father, the blackmailer. She repeated the words to herself over and over as she sank down in a corner of the shower and let the water descend on her in sheets. She felt so dirty. For the first time in her life she felt dirty and she didn't know what on earth she could possibly do to make herself feel clean again. Nik had torn the safe foundations of her very childhood from her.

Her mother, who had died when Leah was four, was no more than a dim memory. The daughter of a minor

English aristocrat, she had been cut off by her family for marrying Max. Max had never told his daughter why. He had never felt the need to explain himself.

Leah's childhood had consisted of a procession of nannies followed by a succession of boarding-schools from an early age. Max had travelled incessantly. Whenever she had pleaded with him to let her live with him, he had always had a ready excuse. She had reached adolescence before she finally appreciated that she was excess baggage in her father's life and he was essentially a remote, self-contained and cold man. None the less she had always been aware that he cared about her as he cared about nobody else.

He had been proud of her beauty, her education, her musical gifts. Those had all been saleable social commodities, she registered now. Max had been ambitious for her. He had wanted her to marry a man of wealth and position. He had always lived on the fringes of high society. He had been keen for his daughter to achieve a passport *into* that same society. Leah had grown up denied the warmth of family life but cocooned from harsh realities. Dependancy had been bred into her bones, along with a desperate need to win her father's love and approval.

How could she ever have guessed that Max was not a legitimate business man? How could she ever have dreamt that her privileged upbringing had been financed by something so vile as the contents of that safety-deposit box? And how could she have even begun to suspect that he had blackmailed Nik into marrying her?

Finally she understood the cruel charade of her marriage, too late for her to do anything any differently. The five years had gone, couldn't be reclaimed either for her or for Nik. No wonder he despised her; no wonder he was so willing to believe that she knew the secret he had been prepared to go to extraordinary lengths to conceal. 'To protect my family', he'd said.

Ironically, she didn't want to know the source of the pressure put on him.

He could keep that skeleton in the closet forever. In any case, Nik's family were strangers to her. He had a mother and three sisters whom she had never met. She had often wondered whether they wondered about her and how Nik had explained so peculiar a marital relationship. But had he even bothered to explain? Like Max, Nik was not in the habit of explaining himself unless he chose to do so.

How could he think she *loved* him? The ultimate humiliation. Not only a husband forced virtually at the point of a gun into marrying her, but a male convinced that even after five years of his excruciating neglect, indifference and infidelity she still loved him! The wife from hell who would cling like a limpet through thick and thin.

Yet as the water continued to beat down on her, Leah slowly began to register a curious sense of burgeoning inner strength which she had never felt before. She even managed to feel sorry for Nik. He was afraid that she intended to try and employ her father's blackmail beyond the grave... hence all the threats, the bullying, the intimidation. The news that she was in love with another man and couldn't wait to get a divorce would surely be manna from heaven, a bolt of joyous blue across Nik's horizon!

She had wasted five years of her life... not one hour, not one day more would she sacrifice! Her father had once been her sole authority. She had allowed Nik to take over that role. Without any argument, she had tolerated Nik's behaviour, even protected him sooner than let her father know that she had not been able to make a success of her marriage. Pride had done that, stupid pride.

And she had been *afraid*, afraid of so much for so long. Afraid of leaving her safe cocoon of monied privilege to face the outside world. Afraid of her father's contempt and fury. Afraid that the truth about her marriage might literally kill her father with his weak heart. No more fear, she told herself now.

If Nik had been a victim, she had been too. And at least she wasn't making as much noise about it as he was, she reflected grimly. His conceit still staggered her. Did he really think that that tender first love of a particularly naïve teenager had outlasted the first six months?

A loud knock sounded on the door.

'Open it!' Nik demanded roughly.

Mentally she blocked her ears. She had had enough of him for one day...enough of him forever. She tasted the concept, and experienced a surge of positively heady relief. Nik did not possess a single virtue which appealed to her. Five years ago it had been an attraction of total opposites on her side. Sweet seventeen, choosing with her heart and her leaping pulses, not with her head.

'Leah!' Nik raked with driven impatience.

He was not a male who respected her sex. He pursued one bimbo after another. Brunette, redhead, blonde. He didn't discriminate. But they all had motorway-length legs, bounteous breasts and big hair. Leah possessed none of those attributes and once that had been a source of torment to her, damaging an already weak self-image.

But she was worth so much more than that and she had Paul to thank for that discovery. Paul had woken her up from her slough of inadequacy and passive acceptance. Paul had taught her to put herself first. The way Nik did; the way Nik had always done. Nik had rejected and humiliated her from the outset of their marriage. What did she have to feel guilty about now? Hadn't she already paid for her father's sins? And the payments in terms of her pain, loneliness and misery stopped now for all time, she swore to herself.

Standing up, switching off the shower, she was in the act of reaching for a towel when the door was suddenly struck with shocking force. The lock buckled and gave, the door slamming back on its hinges, framing Nik in the doorway. His lean, powerful body whipcord-taut, he glowered at her with eyes of flaming jet.

'What did you lock yourself in here for?' he demanded ferociously.

Clutching her towel to her small, slender frame, Leah was shattered by his violent intrusion but she was also furious. 'Have you gone out of your mind?'

White teeth flashed against sun-bronzed skin, his narrowed gaze outraged. 'I was concerned for your welfare!'

Her welfare? Or her safety? Was that why he had kicked down the door like the Neanderthal he was? Had he been afraid that she planned to throw herself out the window? Of course that might have been embarrassing for him.

Dealing him a veiled glance of disbelief, Leah stopped to gather up her discarded clothes.

'Your skin has the bloom of a camellia.'

Her lashes lifted slowly as she straightened. She blinked. Nik was staring at her in the most unbelievably disturbing way, his veiled gaze working intently over every exposed inch of flesh in view, resting on her full mouth, lingering unapologetically on the pale swell of her breasts above the towel.

'Drop the towel,' he said thickly.

Shocked into rigidity, Leah quivered with incredulity. Nik regarded her expectantly. And he was expecting that towel just to drop at his request. It was written all over him, in every poised line of his lounging stance.

Unintentionally, she collided with burning black eyes and it was like having a blowtorch turned on her. Her mouth ran dry, her lungs struggled for oxygen. Heat flamed over her skin as it tightened over her bones, a tiny twisting sensation spiralling through her stomach.

Her breasts felt peculiar, suddenly heavy and full, her nipples tautening into almost painful sensitivity.

'You're so tiny and yet so perfectly proportioned,' he mused lazily in the pulsing silence.

Leah just couldn't believe that he was talking to her like this. And yet on some subconscious level she wasn't surprised. This was Nik as she had never known him and yet as she had always known he could be. There was something dangerously fascinating about the raw sexual charge that emanated from him, the elemental atavism of a very physical male. A 'predator', he had called himself with astonishing candour. And a predator he was, she registered.

'Would you please excuse me while I get dressed?' she murmured without any expression at all.

'You are not serious?' he breathed, as if she were the one behaving oddly.

Leah shivered with fury, disgust flooding through her in waves. Nothing but bitterness, loathing and resentment lay between them but Nik could obviously rise above all that to think about sex. Why? Purely because she was half-naked. Seemingly that was all it took to stoke the ever glowing coals of Nik's powerful libido.

'I want to get dressed,' she said shakily.

'You're shy.' Nik tasted the word with purring satisfaction. 'And you have waited one hell of a long time for me.'

Leah laughed. She couldn't help it. Laughter with an hysterical edge just spilled from her strained lips, shattering the silence like breaking glass.

'Stop it . . .'

Her clothes fell from her arms as she turned away and covered her contorted face with spread hands that were trembling. The hysteria had come from nowhere and attacked without warning. She was furious that he should witness her loss of control. But she was even more devastated when she felt his arms close round her from behind. For a split-second she was so rigid that she imagined herself cracking under the stress of shock and breaking into pieces.

He was pulling her back into the hard, masculine heat of his body, threatening her with a disturbing physical contact she had never had. And she couldn't believe that he was actually touching her. It was so unreal. For five years this man had treated her like a leper. And now all of a sudden, when she was least equipped to deal with him, he was reaching out and touching as though that were his right. But it was not his right and she did not want his hands on her.

'Maybe you don't know where that certificate is,' Nik conceded half under his breath, lowering his dark head. 'Maybe he destroyed it, overlooked the copy. But maybe it's still out there in somebody's safekeeping, like a bomb waiting to be activated...'

His terminology made Leah shiver. Nik was slowly, smoothly turning her round to face him. She had never fully appreciated how much stronger than a woman a man could be until Nik, impatient of her unresponsiveness, simply lifted her clear off the carpet and spun her like a doll back to him.

Barefoot she didn't even reach his shoulder and before he lowered her back down again her cheek brushed against his silk shirt-front as his jacket parted. Her breath caught in her throat, her nostrils flaring at the male scent of him, clean, citrusy... hot. For a timeless moment her senses spun wildly, her lashes dipping as she was flooded by dizzy discomfiture.

'Look at me...' His accented voice could sound like sandpaper on silk.

'Please let me go,' she mumbled in a rush as she relocated her tongue.

She might as well not have spoken. Long fingers tilted up her chin and lingered there as she was involuntarily ensnared by his blazing black eyes. And she knew as clearly as though he had spoken that the seething tension of the afternoon's events and his subsequent furious dissatisfaction had all been temporarily tossed on a back burner. Far more basic urges were driving Nik now, a desire to vent all that pent-up tension in a fashion which she suddenly sensed would come as naturally to him as breathing.

Her skin prickled with a depth of awareness she would not have believed possible. The vibrations in the atmosphere were explosive.

'Nik...' Her own voice emerged jerkily and she wanted to back off fast but her feet were somehow welded to the carpet.

'It's so long since I heard you speak my name...' His intonation was deep-pitched, disturbingly rough, lush ebony lashes low on a sliver of smouldering jet.

'No...' she heard herself whisper.

His thumb smoothed along the voluptuous curve of her lower lip and she trembled, attempted to move, but his other hand was splayed across her taut spine, holding her steady.

He watched her intently as he prised her lips apart with his thumb, intruded into the soft, damp interior, making her shiver violently as his palm cupped her delicate jawbone. It was the most insidiously erotic gesture she had ever experienced, and set up a terrifying chain reaction through her treacherous body.

He was playing with her, tracking her every tiny response with a mixture of satisfaction and amusement. And she understood that, read that in the eyes made famous by the financial press for being 'as unreadable as a blackout'.

But he wasn't testing the water...no, indeed. Nik was neither humble nor uncertain. This was a male wholly acquainted with every seductive and sensual technique necessary to heighten his own pleasure and a male, similarly given over to taking that pleasure whenever the mood took him.

'I want——' And her tongue felt too large for her mouth.

'More?' With devastating abruptness but immense cool, Nik released her and angled a sizzling smile down at her. 'Next time, drop the towel when I ask, *pethi mou*,' he advised softly.

She would have found a blow less degrading than that insolent conclusion. As she heard the bedroom door snap quietly shut in his wake, Leah went limp, her pallor pronounced. She had challenged him, angered him. She was shattered. All these years, nothing, and then...

Why now? She remembered him saying that her father could not force him into her bed as he had forced him into marriage. Her stomach twisted painfully. Max was dead now. And she had been available... in so much as she was *female*. Seemingly it took little else to attract Nik when he was in the mood for a little light sexual relief.

And the peculiar way he had made her feel... But then that had been sheer shock and nervous paralysis, Leah told herself urgently. She had only been doing the sensible thing in not fighting, not arguing. Nik was Greek and macho to the backbone. Telling him just at that moment either that she wanted a divorce or that she could not bear him to lay a single finger upon her might have been received like a thrown gauntlet and it might well have encouraged him to attempt further intimacies.

No, that had definitely not been the right moment to mention Paul.

Leah climbed back into her clothes, conscious that her hands were clumsy and still not quite steady. But then that was hardly surprising. Her husband had finally chosen to notice that she was alive... well, if not quite alive at least physically capable of providing the kind of entertainment he expected from her sex. She was disgusted, absolutely disgusted by his brazen disregard for decency in even daring to approach her!

Not only did he have no right to touch her, he wasn't even faithful to whomever he was currently sharing a bed with. And if she had been willing she had not the slightest doubt that Nik would have taken advantage of her willingness. He was made that way. A taker, not a giver.

He had had a hard fight building his father's holdings up into the vast international power base that was the Andreakis heritage today. Nobody had given Nik any favours...so he gave none back. He went after his enemies like a warlord, slaughtered them and came back primitively victorious. He hid no light under a bushel, left no stone unturned in his fight for supremacy.

And it was all those traits which her father had gloried in and dished up to her in suitable euphemisms to persuade her that though Nik had made no mention of love he would make her a wonderful husband.

Her mouth curved downwards in grim amusement. What husband? She had never had a husband. But five years ago she hadn't had the benefit of a crystal ball...

Doubtless memory failed her for her recollection of their first meeting was radically different from his. Before that day, Leah had neither seen nor heard of Nik Andreakis. She had just completed one term at finishing school, perfecting her technique with stupid flower arrangements... A course on *men* would have been far more useful, she reflected now.

Nik had appeared in the doorway of the conservatory, uninvited and unexpected. The maid had put him in the drawing-room to wait for her father and he must have seen her through the window because to get to the conservatory he had had to leave the drawing-room, cross the hall, go through another room and enter the conservatory by the French windows there. So how come he'd accused her of setting *him* up for a meeting?

She had looked up and seen him in the doorway and, yes, at one glance had fallen head over heels in love with him. Nik had struck her as the most utterly gorgeous creation she had ever seen walk on two feet. He had stood there like a golden Greek god and her knees had wobbled, helpless excitement quivering through her.

'You are a breath of spring in this winter scene,' he had drawled almost stiltedly, dark eyes literally riveted to her.

Yes, he had said it—probably read it somewhere and memorised it for effect, but those most un-Nik-like words had indeed emerged from him. Her pruning scissors had dropped from her nerveless fingers. He had picked them up and hovered. Yes, definitely hovered, as though one part of him was urging him to retreat and another urging him to stay.

It had never occurred to Leah that he had deliberately sought her out. She had assumed that he was interested in the plants and a conversation that years on should have filled her with hilarity but somehow failed to do so had taken place. Nik had not revealed either his ignorance or his uninterest. He had asked appropriate questions and contrived to conceal the fact that he had undoubtedly never touched or examined a plant in his life before.

He had even told her that her eyes matched the gentian violets, and that compliment had emerged almost as awkwardly as the first, giving Leah the impression that though he looked staggeringly sophisticated he was almost shy. *Shy*? *Nik*?

How much time had gone by in that conservatory? He hadn't mentioned his appointment with her father, indeed had given all the appearance of having forgotten it until the flustered maid had come in search of Leah to tell her that her father wanted her and had been disconcerted to find Nik with her.

'I'll·tell him you're waiting,' Leah had told him, and she had flown upstairs to her father's library.

'Who is he?' she had asked straight off, after giving the kind of description that had probably sounded like something that leapt off the page of one of the torrid romances that she had then been so fond of.

'Nik Andreakis...' Max had surveyed her glowing face with cool, narrowed eyes.

'He's been here absolutely ages,' she had burbled. 'Don't you think we should ask him to stay to dinner?'

'He appears to have been quite a hit.'

'Is he married?'

And Nik had duly been invited—her fault, entirely her fault. Her father had come down to make his apologies and then left them alone and Nik had spent all the time before dinner asking her about herself. He had had no need to wonder whether she was over the age of consent. She had told him exactly what age she was...and he had visibly winced...

The following day he had taken her out for a drive but Max had been very dubious about it and she'd suspected that Nik had been made embarrassingly aware of the fact that her father was extremely protective of her.

'I think your father may have you dusted for fingerprints when you go home, so I won't kiss you,' he had said drily. 'I don't know what I'm doing here with you. You're far too young for me.'

And she had been hurt, terribly hurt in the week that followed, when he'd neither phoned nor visited. Max had been coolly amused by her misery and had wryly told her not to wear her heart on her sleeve.

'Andreakis can have just about any woman he wants,' he had volunteered. 'But I don't want him around you unless he's got marriage in mind.'

'And did you tell him that?' she had gasped in horror.

'You may not value yourself but I do,' her father had retorted crushingly. 'I sent you to the finest schools to

ensure that you could take your place in any company.
I want you to marry well, Leah. A sordid little fling with
Andreakis is not on your agenda. And you can be assured that he won't offer anything more unless it's
profitable.'

Nik had shown up unexpectedly the second week,
moody and almost aggressive in his attitude towards her.
He had stayed to dinner again. Max had been in an un-
usually good mood but quiet, very quiet, watching them
both, adding little to the conversation.

Two days after that her father had called her into his
library and calmly informed her that he owned a considerable number of shares in a shipping line called
Petrakis International, shares which Nik was extremely
keen to acquire.

'So I offered them to him gratis as a wedding present,'
Max had smoothly concluded.

Leah had been appalled and deeply upset. Yes, she
had been crazy about Nik but that her father should
have coolly approached him and offered him a bribe to
marry her had made her feel sick with humiliation.

'Nik's Greek. He understands these kinds of arrangements,' Max had assured her witheringly. 'And I suggest
that *you* understand that a man as tough as Nik
Andreakis wouldn't even consider marriage unless it was
financially advantageous. Those shares could be your
dowry. The choice is yours. Do you want him or don't
you?'

She had run out of the room, choked with the sobs
of her distress. The next morning Max had informed her
quite unemotionally of his heart condition. He had said
that he didn't know how long he had left and he was
very worried about what would happen to her if he died
in the near future. Leah had been shattered by the news.

He had praised Nik to the skies. Nik might be something of a rough diamond by virtue of his hard upbringing but he would treat her with respect and honour

as his wife. Such marriage arrangements were common in Greece. If she married Nik she would be safe, secure for the . . . *for the rest of her life*. As that phrase returned to haunt her, Leah searched her ashen reflection in the bedroom mirror.

'But he doesn't love me!' she had protested.

Max had looked at her with icy contempt. 'He *wants* you . . .'

'Not as much as he wants those blasted shares,' she had whispered strickenly.

'It's up to you what you make of the marriage. I'm giving you the chance to marry the man you love . . .'

Leah came fully back to the present and clasped her cold hands together. I'm giving you Nik Andreakis on a silver platter, Max might as well have said. She shuddered with distaste, despising her own naïveté. Nik had been delivered to her handcuffed and chained by blackmail and even Max hadn't pretended that love had anything to do with it. Where had her intelligence been?

A knock sounded on the door. It was a servant announcing dinner. Leah was shaken. Could it really be that time already? Paul phoned her at eight every evening. He knew she never went out at night. Would Petros have told him that she was in Paris? She lifted the phone by the bed and dialled the number of his apartment. The call was answered almost immediately.

'Where the hell are you?' Paul demanded sharply. 'Petros told me that Mr and Mrs Andreakis were "unavailable". What the heck is that supposed to mean?'

'We had to fly to Paris——'

'*We*?' he interrupted, an octave higher.

'Look, there was a problem with Max's estate and I had to be with him,' Leah framed tautly. 'I'll be home tomorrow, darling. I love you.'

'What sort of a problem?' Paul sounded very edgy.

'Nothing important,' she said breathlessly. No way did she intend to unload the sordid revelations Nik had forced her to endure on Paul. At least not on the phone...and not yet, she adjusted, reminding herself that a strong relationship needed to be based on honesty and trust.

'Good...so is he taking you out to see the joys of Paris?' Paul mocked.

'Nik...take me out? You've got to be kidding.' She forced a laugh, relieved that he wasn't angry any more. 'I miss you so much. I haven't stopped thinking about you for a second.'

'Tomorrow can't come soon enough,' he swore.

'I can't wait...but I can't use Charlie's again,' she abruptly recalled, her nervous tension rocketing as she wondered frantically how she was going to ditch Boyce, short of swinging out of her bedroom window on a rope like Tarzan's Jane.

Charlie had had a point, she acknowledged unhappily. She wasn't cut out for this game of sneaking around. She so badly wanted everything to be above board. No matter how much her intelligence told her that she was not a married woman except on paper—which she told herself on a very regular basis—her conscience reminded her that she had taken her vows in a church and had meant them at the time she made them.

'Why not ask him for the divorce? Use the opportunity,' Paul suggested meaningfully. 'Stop being such a coward. The guy is totally indifferent to you. Why should he care?'

A tiny sound sent Leah's head flying up. A surge of bone-chilling horror paralysed her to the spot—but not before she dropped the phone with a clatter.

She had forgotten to close the door again. Nik stood there, as incredibly still and silent as a centuries-old statue. Literally traumatised by the sight, Leah stared back at him with very wide sapphire-blue eyes as if he had just dropped down through the ceiling without warning.

Nik...she tried to say lightly, but when she opened her dry mouth no sound emerged at all.

'Dinner...' he murmured smoothly, and smiled. 'But finish your call first.'

Reaching down, she fumbled for the phone. 'Bye,' she said, and cut the connection.

CHAPTER THREE

HER heart hammering wildly behind her breastbone, Leah watched Nik swing on his heel and depart and then all her muscles gave and she was ready to flop with almost sick relief. He couldn't have heard anything. He would have said something if he had...wouldn't he? Or reacted in some way, which he hadn't. He had actually smiled.

As she left the bedroom, fighting to regain her smashed composure, she heard the manservant tell Nik that the car was waiting. As she neared the hall, she heard Nik cancel it. Had he been planing to dine out and then changed his mind? Well, she certainly hoped he wasn't staying in for her benefit. A little voice told her how exceedingly unlikely it was that Nik would do anything for her benefit.

'I have some calls of my own to make,' Nik delivered in a flat aside as she drew almost level. 'Don't wait for me.'

Leah ate without even being aware of what she was eating. She felt guilty, enervated, dismayingly confused. Her temples throbbed with strain. All her life she had been open and honest...well, that was until three short months ago when Paul had accidentally sent her flying in Harrods. Deception was abhorrent to her but it hadn't occurred to her at the outset that she would become involved with him. He had insisted on taking her into the restaurant. They had laughed and chatted over coffee. Nothing could have been more innocent. The second meeting had been entirely accidental as well...

Pushing her plate away, Leah gulped down a glass of wine but it didn't take the nasty taste from her mouth.

Why on earth did she feel like this? All she had to do was ask Nik for a divorce soon and it would all be over. Maybe she should stop seeing Paul until then. Was that what she should be doing? Or maybe she should just walk out and leave Nik a note to find the next time he was in London. Cowardly, but probably all he deserved.

She was quite sure that Nik hadn't agonised over any of *his* women. He certainly hadn't cared about Leah's feelings. Leah had had to live with humiliation in newsprint as well as in private. Nik was extremely photogenic and a gossip columnist's dream, the married man who led the adulterer's dream existence without any apparent interference from his wife. For Nik to say that he had been on a leash for five years was errant nonsense. But then two wrongs did not make a right. Why should she stoop to Nik's level?

Deciding against coffee, the exhaustion of extreme stress creeping over her like a suffocating blanket, Leah decided to go to bed. Her strained mouth compressed when she remembered that she had no nightwear. The towelling robe hung in the bathroom for the use of guests was too bulky for comfort. In the end she slid naked between the smooth percale sheets and in the comforting darkness she reached a decision. Tomorrow morning she would tell Nik that she wanted a divorce. Then there would be no further need for her over-active conscience to torment her with this ridiculous sense of being in the wrong.

She awakened from a deep sleep with a start. The overhead lights were on full and she blinked in complete disorientation as she sat up, momentarily not even recalling where she was. And then her sleepy eyes focused on Nik where he was poised several feet from the bed and flew wide. He looked like hell; that was her first thought as she clutched the sheet protectively round herself, belatedly recalling her nudity.

His luxuriant black hair was tousled, his tie was missing and the white silk dress-shirt he wore beneath his dinner-jacket was half-open, displaying a disturbing wedge of bronzed chest, liberally sprinkled with curling dark whorls of hair. His strong, dark features were fiercely clenched and for someone of his usually vibrant skintone he was staggeringly pale. Almost as though he was in shock, she thought uncertainly...severe shock.

"Wh—what's wrong...what time is it?' she mumbled, pushing a hand through the silken disarray of the silvery hair falling round her shoulders, swallowing back a yawn as she glanced at her watch to discover that it was the early hours of the morning.

'You have dishonoured my name,' Nik breathed in what sounded more like broken English by virtue of the unusual thickness of his accent and his decidedly rough delivery.

Leah cleared her throat and looked back at him, still not quite awake, fighting through the fog of her slow reactions. Eyes as black as pitch clashed on a violent collision course with hers and the explosive tension emanating from him in electrifying waves was finally communicated to her.

'Excuse me?' she muttered, certain that he couldn't possibly have said what she had thought he had said.

'My wife with another man...' He could hardly get the words out as he continued to stare at her with un-wavering force as though she were some alien entity he had never seen before.

Ghostly fingers danced up her taut spinal cord. She tried and failed to swallow. But what ironically struck Leah hardest was not his evident discovery that she had been seeing another man but that truly staggering des-ignation of 'my wife', a label which until now Nik had never once been heard to voice. In turn, Leah found that same label almost unbelievably offensive, not to mention ridiculous in the context of their marriage.

'You do not deny it,' Nik murmured, every powerful angle of his lean body rigid with raw tension.

Leah hugged the sheet, wondering dazedly why he was so incensed. For shock she should have read disbelief. Had he expected her to sit there like some wet, faithful Penelope forever, watching her life drain away into nothingness? All right, so she had been a doormat for a very long time, but surely even Nik could not have expected that to last indefinitely? And, in any case, what was it to him?

'How did you find out?' she asked, not as steadily as she would have liked, but fighting the intimidation of his dark, menacing attitude with all her strength.

'You do not even seem to appreciate the magnitude of your offence.' Nik studied her with outraged dark eyes and, if possible, he was even paler than he had been minutes earlier.

'Have you been drinking?' Leah prompted weakly, wondering if that was what lay at the foot of such utterly unwarranted melodrama. Coming into her room in the middle of the night, confronting her like a wronged husband . . . how could he possibly consider himself wronged?

'What the hell has that to do with anything?' Moving an unwelcome step closer, Nik abruptly spread two lean hands in a violent arc of eloquent expression. 'I hear you on the phone with your lover. What I hear I cannot believe!'

'Oh.' Leah bent her head. She should have guessed. But Nik was so naturally devious, he hadn't given a sign at the time. She tried to recall what she had said but she couldn't, the conversation having been rushed and overshadowed by Nik's appearance. Well, she thought, sucking in a deep breath, it wouldn't have been the way she would have chosen for Nik to find out, but maybe it was for the best that it was all finally out in the open.

'I had the London phone bills faxed to me and then I used the redial facility on the phone you had employed and checked it against the number you call most frequently.'

Devious didn't begin to describe him. An odd squirming sensation afflicted Leah and she fought it, glancing up to say tightly, 'I would have told you about him if you had asked.'

'*Told me about him*? *Cristo*...do you have no shame?'

Her chin came up. 'Why should I be ashamed?' But for some inexplicable reason his attitude was having that effect on her and that made her angry.

'You...are...my...wife,' Nik spelt out with a flash of even white teeth and an aura of pure violence, on the brink of being unleashed.

Instinctively, Leah edged across to the far side of the bed, assailed by bewilderment and something that was coming perilously close to fear in spite of her anger. When he said she was his wife she wanted to scream back at him that she was no more his wife than a stranger in the street but his mood forestalled her. He was scaring her. She didn't want to risk adding fuel to the fire.

'Perhaps you'll be feeling more reasonable in the morning.' She placed gentle stress on the last three words.

'Why?' Nik demanded in a low, seething undertone, striding round the bed. 'Why would I be feeling more reasonable?'

As Leah attempted to repeat the evasive manoeuvre she had utilised mere seconds earlier, Nik disconcerted her entirely by suddenly coming down on the bed and clamping a bruising hand round her arm to hold her in place.

'What are you doing?' she shrieked in sudden panic.

He spat something in Greek at her and pinned her down by her other arm as well when she attempted to pull free. White as a sheet, her teeth chattering with shock, she gazed up at him with frightened eyes.

Blazing black eyes bit down into her. 'How often have you been with him?'

'I . . . I didn't count.' Her mind was a total terrified blank.

'*Theos.*' Nik intoned with vicious intent. 'I will kill him . . . I will wipe him from the face of this earth! He's dead. He may still be walking around but he is dead.'

'Don't s-say things like that!' Leah gasped in horror.

'And what about you? What do I do with you?'

'*Me*?' On the edge of hysteria and frozen there, Leah stared up at him aghast. He was unhinged. That was the only possible explanation.

'Where did you meet him?'

'I'm not telling you anything about him!' she asserted, shivering as she recalled his threats.

'Paul Stephen Woods. He's twenty-eight. He's a would-be artist, part-time salesman. He's an only child, blond, blue-eyed, six feet tall and he is very ambitious. I don't need you to tell me any of that.'

Leah was transfixed. The tip of her tongue snaked out to moisten her dry lips. She trembled. 'Why are you behaving like this? Why should it matter to you? I'm not your wife—not really your wife . . .'

'*Ohi* . . . no?' he probed dangerously. 'You carry my name. You wear my ring. You live in my house. I feed you, I clothe you, I keep you.'

Mortified beyond bearing, Leah reddened fiercely. 'And I hate you!'

'If that is true, you will hate me a lot more by the time I am finished,' Nik responded darkly in the pulsating silence.

'Let me go,' she whispered shakily.

'You will never see him again,' he swore, his eyes smouldering down at her in barely leashed rage. In a sudden fluid movement he shifted back from her, releasing her arms. 'But I will never forgive you for this . . .'

Feeling weak as a kitten, she slumped back against the pillows. Her reply just leapt off her tongue. 'That's OK,' she said. 'I'll never forgive you either.'

It was a mistake. Halfway to the door, Nik stilled and spun back. 'So *now* you tell me the truth.'

'What truth?'

'That this is a deliberate attempt to attract my attention,' he condemned with splintering fury. 'No wonder you left tracks a blind man could follow... no wonder I am treated to an open door and the sound of you exchanging sweet nothings with your lover!'

'Attract *your* attention?' Leah repeated, her exquisite face alight with unhidden incredulity, physical weakness banished as she sat up in one abrupt movement.

'Which you have done beautifully,' Nik conceded with a sudden blazing smile that chilled her to the marrow. 'You haven't even slept with him, have you? So far and no further. Perfect.' He strolled back towards the bed, riveting dark eyes probing her with derisive brilliance. 'Not enough to send me over the edge but enough to make me sit back and take notice...'

Momentarily she was stunned by the sheer depth of his conceit. Then she flung her head back, sapphire eyes flashing with fury. 'I *have* slept with him!' she lied hotly. 'And I don't want you over the edge or taking notice because I don't give a damn about you!'

'If he has laid one finger on your unclothed body, he's dead. You do understand that?' Nik surveyed her with hooded dark eyes, a lethal stillness to his lean, powerful body. 'This is not some game. I warn you, *pethi mou*. If he's had you, I'll break him,' he asserted with murderous cool.

Leah couldn't move, couldn't breathe, couldn't credit that he could back her into a corner like that. And how could he possibly guess that her relationship with Paul had yet to become intimate? She had lied in temper but also out of a need to stress that it was a serious relationship, not some silly flirtation manufactured to attract an indifferent husband's attention. The very suggestion that she might be guilty of such childishly manipulative, not to say pathetic behaviour made her blood boil in her veins. But she was simultaneously terrified that Nik might harm Paul.

'You are having to think so hard about this, I feel almost embarrassed,' Nik revealed smoothly.

And all the anger had gone as if it had never been, she registered in a daze. 'OK,' she muttered tightly, studying her tightly linked hands, hating Nik with so much venom that she was literally ill with the force of her feelings. 'I haven't slept with him but——'

'And shall I tell you why? A Greek would divorce an unfaithful wife. So you went as far as you dared and no further. The only reckless thing you ever did in your life was marry me. *Cristo*.' Nik expelled his breathe in a hiss. 'What a fool I was to think for one second that you might risk losing your status as my wife!'

'But that's exactly what I want to lose!' Leah shot back at him in untrammelled rage and frustration. 'I don't want you... I want my freedom!'

'Like hell you do,' Nik responded crushingly. 'You'd sink like a stone in the real world. You couldn't cut it out there. You'd be as helpless as a newborn baby without your credit cards!'

'How dare you?' Leah spat, white as snow.

A winged ebony brow elevated. 'I was just telling it like it is. You are exactly what Max created: a beautiful, fragile ornament, the perfect wife for a very rich man, born to be waited on hand and foot...'

'You swine,' she gasped, pain tearing through her in a blinding wave.

'That's not to say that you're not very good in your own rarefied milieu,' he drawled in wry addition. 'You're a marvellous hostess. And you're a real lady. But if you really want your freedom——'

'I do!' Leah practically sobbed at him.

'Ask yourself why you're still buying my socks.' Unleashing a sardonic smile on her, Nik turned and strode out of the room.

What did his bloody socks have to do with anything? That was just a trivial task she had taken on early in their marriage and kept on doing without even thinking about it! Leah dived out of bed, snatching up the towelling robe and digging her arms frantically into it. She had to make him listen. She had to make him understand.

He was in the master bedroom. Leah halted on the threshold, discomfited to find him halfway out of his shirt.

'What now?' he grated with driven impatience.

'I want you to listen to me.' Twitching the neck of the robe higher with restive fingertips, she made herself meet his unreadable gaze. 'I love Paul. I want a divorce.'

Nik strolled across the depth of the carpet towards her. 'You're my wife,' he delivered in a soft tone of revelation. 'And why are you my wife? Because you so badly wanted to be my wife.'

A hectic flush ran up her slender throat and her teeth clenched. 'Did you hear what I said? I *love* him!'

'You're buying his socks too?' Nik enquired without pause, savage amusement in his narrowed scrutiny.

Without her even thinking about it, her hand flashed up and she slapped him hard, so hard that she couldn't feel her fingers for several taut seconds afterwards. Then she was shocked by what she had done, the unfamiliar violence which had simply surged up out of nowhere and spilt over. Fearfully, she flinched back from him as he reached out for her, all amusement banished from his hard, dark eyes.

'No!'

'Even when I think a bloody good slap might do you good I can restrain myself. You're too small, too breakable. If I'd been the wife-beating type, don't you think you would have known it by now?'

Nik tugged her resistant body closer with easy strength, another kind of threat entirely explicit in the slow-burn effect of his dark gaze wandering over her, lingering on the steadily widening V of pale skin revealed by the far too large robe as it slid down off one narrow-boned shoulder.

'And I have to confess that my idea of entertainment is rather more intimate than violence and infinitely more satisfying.'

'Don't you dare touch me!' Leah screeched so loudly that her voice cracked and her throat hurt.

'A long, hot night in my bed is exactly what you need.' A lean hand settled on her bare shoulder.

'Don't be disgusting!' Leah's facial muscles locked with revulsion.

'And don't dismiss out of hand what you have never experienced.' Nik laughed softly as he lowered his darkly handsome head and dragged her relentlessly up against him, one hand curving to the swell of her hips.

'Stop it——'

'I feel so threatened,' he mocked indolently, brushing a silvery strand of hair back from one delicate cheekbone in an almost tender gesture that struck her as so out of character that she found herself briefly losing track of her struggle for freedom.

'Nik...'

His mouth came down on hers with mesmerising expertise and prised her soft lips apart. She stopped breathing. He gathered her closer, sealing her to every abrasively male angle of his taut body. Her back arched without her volition, increasing that contact. His tongue drove into the moist, tender interior she had yielded and explored. A river of fire flowed through her and she quivered, leaning against him, winding her arms sinuously round his neck. Darkness beckoned behind her lowered eyelids, the heat in the pit of her stomach twisting like a hot wire through her trembling length.

Nik freed her swollen mouth and studied her with complete impassivity. 'What was his name?' he derided.

'His...oh, God!' On unsteady legs, Leah went into retreat, her fingers flying up in stark distress and turmoil to her reddened lips.

'''Frailty, thy name is woman!''' Nik quoted with savage amusement. 'But you've got your priorities wrong. I'm the husband.'

Leah struggled to think of something—anything to say in self-defence. Nothing occurred to her. As she hovered, prey to a number of conflicting violent emotions, Nik shed his shirt, displaying powerful muscles that rippled like flexing cords beneath his golden skin. She didn't want to stare but she stared all the same.

Nik moved past her, opened the door and thrust her unceremoniously out into the corridor, murmuring, 'We'll talk over breakfast.'

The door thudded shut in her confused face. Was she going out of her mind? Had the past twenty-four tension-filled hours been a nightmare? She got back into bed, curled up in the foetal position and hugged herself. Nik was a stranger. She didn't know him like this...and just for a little while she hadn't known herself either.

He had been so bitter, so enraged at the bank. He had devastated her. But since then his every switch of mood had caught her by surprise. It was as if there were a script running somewhere and she was the only one who hadn't read it yet.

He had seethed with rage when he'd realised that she had been seeing another man. He had scared her half out of her wits. But as long as the affair had been ar-rested outside the bedroom door he was able to shrug it off with the truly astonishing belief that she had only been trying to make him sit up and take notice of her. And all of a sudden he was being sarcastic rather than furious, assuring her that she couldn't survive except as his wife and revealing with every following word and action the most staggering revelation of all...

Nik didn't seem to want a divorce. And Leah found that totally and absolutely unbelievable in the circumstances. Why would he want to hang on to a wife he had been blackmailed into marrying? Why would he want to hang on to an empty charade?

It didn't make sense; it didn't make any sense at all. Her every expectation had been torn from her and she felt like somebody trying to walk a tightrope in the dark. Nik was volatile, unpredictable...OK. But this was something else again and she couldn't sleep for wondering what was motivating him and why all of a sudden he was making sexual advances to a wife he had blithely ignored for five years.

Even worse was trying to figure out why she hadn't fought him off, why she had just stood there and allowed him to kiss her... and felt so hot and wanton that she could have died with shame afterwards. Nik was very experienced. Maybe any male, possessed of that brand of carnal expertise, could tempt a woman as inexperienced as she was. Maybe it was all a matter of pressing the right physical buttons. Even so, he had still dragged a response from her far more powerful than Paul had ever managed.

Don't, she screamed inside her head, guilty and thoroughly ashamed of herself. How could there be any comparison? Sex was the least important thing in a relationship, to her way of thinking. She loved Paul; she *did* love Paul. Nik had shaken that belief not at all.

But she was badly shaken by the unwelcome discovery that she could still be vulnerable after all this time to Nik's undeniable sexual charisma. She had thought she had grown out of that. She had thought she was safe, cured, indifferent. And he had taught her other-

wise...and laughed. Dear God, *laughed*. She relived the
moment, racked by the torment of her shattered pride.

A case was sitting just inside the door when she woke
up, feeling like a corpse. Nik had had fresh clothing
flown in. Oh, so thoughtful of him. Leah donned the
dark blue Versace suit, spent longer than usual striving
to repair the ravages of a virtually sleepless night and
only emerged from the bedroom when she felt she had
achieved the miracle.

Nik was lounging back in his chair behind the *Financial
Times*. He lowered it, cast it aside and lifted his coffee.
'You should go back to bed. You look like a vampire
victim waiting on the third bite.'

'Very funny,' Leah gritted, a flush driving away the
pallor which had made the blusher on her cheeks stand
out.

An ebony brow quirked. 'I think you're incredibly
lucky still to be all in one unbruised, attached piece after
what I found out last night. I think I have been remarkably tolerant and understanding—but don't push
it.'

Leah snatched at a croissant, conscious of night-dark
eyes tracking her every movement. He was etched in her
mind's eye. Immaculate in a navy pinstriped suit and red
silk tie. No bags under his eyes. No visible sign of last
night's horrors marred *his* natural vibrancy. Her nerves
were shattered and he was as laid-back and in control
as he had ever been. In fact he looked bloody smug.
Hatred coursed through her. Her hands shook as she
tore apart the croissant.

'I intend to see a solicitor this morning,' she announced without looking at him. 'I want a divorce.'

'In your dreams,' Nik said softly.

Her silver head shot up. 'I——'

'Shut up,' Nik told her with hard emphasis.

'You can't prevent me.'

'I'll just pretend I didn't hear that.'

'And I'm not going to sit here and be insulted.'

'*Sit down*!' he bit out, his hard voice cracking like a whiplash down the table at her. And Leah got such a shock that she sat again. 'I want you to listen to me.'

She sugared her coffee, refusing to look up. Let him have his say. He was not going to stop her starting a divorce. She was entitled to her freedom and nothing he could do or say was likely to stop her reaching out and simply grabbing it.

'Five years ago I was twenty-five and you were seventeen, a very young seventeen. A child inside a woman's body. And I don't get all hot and excited at the idea of sleeping with an adolescent, even if she is my wife! I found *that* a complete turn-off,' Nik delivered with excruciating candour. 'Some men like very young girls. I'm not one of them.'

Leah kept on stirring her coffee. She was very pale, painfully embarrassed and oddly guilty that it had never once crossed her mind that Nik might feel that way about the teenaged bride he had had forced on him. 'You hated me anyway,' she said tightly.

'I resented you. I don't think I ever got as far as hating you. I just closed you out,' Nik mused. 'We were stuck with each other and I dealt with it my way.'

'Excuse me if I throw up,' Leah inserted jerkily, unable to still the juvenile response but suddenly blatantly conscious of just how juvenile she had sounded. Nor did she want the past raked up, she registered uneasily. There was so much pain and turmoil there. She might have learnt to put it behind her but he was dragging up very raw memories . . .

'I started work when I was fourteen on one of my father's ships. He was an old-fashioned man. He wanted me to start at the bottom and work up because he had done it that way. I knew I needed an education. The next eight years were filled with eighteen-hour days. When I wasn't slogging my guts out I was studying to try and keep up and playing the stock market on the side. I didn't have a misspent youth. I didn't have time for one,' Nik completed drily.

He had never talked to her like this before. It disturbed her. She lifted her coffee-cup and hugged it to her, finding some kind of security in its warmth. She had had a rough idea of what his early years had been like but she hadn't realised they had been quite as grim and joyless as he made them sound. 'I don't know why you're telling me this.'

'I want you to understand what it was like for me being forced into marriage when I wasn't ready for it.'

'I understand perfectly,' Leah said frigidly.

'I had finally reached the top. I was at last free to do everything I never got to do when I was younger,' he asserted in a driven undertone.

'You were free to sleep around,' Leah rephrased with icy distaste. 'And then Max came along and saddled you with me, right?'

'*Theos*,' Nik exclaimed. '*Ne*...yes, if you must put it like that, but I did not sleep around. You're a woman. You couldn't possibly understand what it is like for a man. It is a stage every man has to go through but I went through it later than most.'

Sexist toad, she thought bitterly, drinking down her coffee in one gulp. There was a whole world of gasping, gushing women out there and she sincerely doubted that he had left one willing woman unexplored. Apart from his wife. Leah had been left in frozen animation, denied everything he took by right for himself. Stowed away on a shelf to shrivel up in an empty, echoing London house where even the servants were foreign. A consuming bitterness assailed her.

'I get the picture. As insidious an excuse for adultery as any woman has ever received. In fact, it's so damned brilliant, you really ought to go public with it!'

'I am not apologising for myself. I married you under duress. I would not have married you otherwise. I was not ready to make that commitment to any woman at twenty-five.' Smouldering black eyes smashed into hers with unashamed force. 'It was better that I left you alone than shared your bed and strayed as I probably would have done.'

'I don't doubt it.' Leah was trembling with a combustible mix of emotions: rage, resentment, hatred and remembered pain and humiliation. She physically hurt with the control it took to hold them in.

Nik watched her from below lush ebony lashes. 'And then there was the obscene idea of performing like a stud for Max's benefit.'

Leah reddened as though he had slapped her across the face.

'On many occasions I have looked at you over the last couple of years and been very tempted to take you to my bed but it would have been like surrendering to the enemy and I doubt if you would have enjoyed the effect that had on me.'

'I really don't want to hear any more,' she admitted tightly.

Nik ignored her. 'But now Max is gone. And I may not have that certificate as yet but I don't believe you know where it is . . . or even *what* it is.'

'You wouldn't believe how relieved I feel. Tell me, is there some point to this deeply unpleasant walk down memory lane?' Leah prompted stiffly.

Nik treated her to a wolfish smile. 'I'm ready to settle down into being married.'

Her breath escaped in an audible hiss. Her lashes flickered. Incredulous sapphire-blue eyes clung to his darkly handsome features, her heartbeat sitting somewhere in the neighbourhood of her convulsed throat.

CHAPTER FOUR

'YOU look as if you need a good, stiff drink.' Rising gracefully upright, Nik strode across to the polished antique sideboard, extracted a brandy goblet and calmly poured a measure from the cut-glass decanter. With incredible cool, he settled it down on the table in front of her and strolled across to the marble fireplace.

'You can't be serious,' Leah told him, dry-mouthed.

'Apart from the taint of your family tree, you're everything I want in a wife.'

'Forgive me if I find that impossible to believe.'

'You're beautiful, sexually appealing and you're already mine,' he drawled with wry amusement. 'And I haven't met anyone else one half as suitable.'

'Thanks but no, thanks.' Shaken to her innermost depths by the proposition, Leah was bereft of the wit to come back with anything more sarcastic.

'I don't recall saying you had the right of refusal. And I'm prepared to be reasonable. I proved that last night.' Nik dealt her a razor-sharp glance of explicit meaning. 'I could have flattened you down on my bed there and then——'

'No!' Leah rose upright, rigid with rejection.

'But I didn't. I'll give you time to adjust to the idea. I don't expect you to behave as though the last five years never happened.'

'I love Paul.'

'And I don't expect to hear his name on your lips again. I warned you. That is over. You're allowed one mistake, one vengeful little fling and you've had it.' Nik ran hooded dark eyes grimly over her pale, set face. 'One mistake,' he repeated in case she hadn't got the message. 'Phone him, go near him ever again and I'll break both of you because whether you like it or not you're my wife!'

'You can't do that . . . you can't threaten me!'

'That wasn't a threat, *pethi mou*, that was a cast-iron promise. Cross the boundary lines I set and take the consequences. Don't say you weren't warned,' he murmured with chilling emphasis. 'Don't think that because I was tolerant last night I'll be tolerant again. I won't be.'

'You can't make me stay with you.'

'Try me; step out of line and see what happens,' he invited darkly, scanning her with angry black eyes. 'And don't kid yourself that you've found true love. Woods has a history of chasing wealthy women.'

'He didn't even know I was wealthy!' Leah spat at him furiously.

'He'd have to be blind not to. Look at your jewellery . . . look at your clothes! Why do you think you have a bodyguard? You're a walking invitation for every mugger for miles around! That bracelet on your wrist is worth more than he could earn in a lifetime!' he slashed back rawly. 'And he needn't think you'd be bringing your father's blood money with you because you will be signing your entire inheritance away to charity.'

'Really?' she gasped.

'You want to keep it? Profit from all the misery he caused his victims?'

Sick to the stomach at the idea, Leah slung him a thwarted look of loathing and turned away.

'You return to London and pack. We're flying to Greece in forty-eight hours.'

'Greece?' she echoed.

'It's time you met my family.'

'No way am I staying married to you and no way am I going to Greece!'

'Go take a long, cool shower and concentrate on the absence of options available,' Nik advised drily. 'And when you've finished doing that, think about how long Woods lingered in your dizzy brain when you were in my arms last night.'

'You bastard...' It was a derogatory term she had never used before, a word she had never liked, but it came out all the same.

Nik stilled. 'And why do you call me that?'

She went icy cold under the onslaught of his savage gaze.

'Why?' he persisted.

'Well, why not?' Leah backed away, shocked by the menacing vibrations churning up the atmosphere around them. 'You swine...' she fumbled stupidly.

'I can live with that one.' His intense gaze veiled, his expressive mouth compressing. 'Leah...we could have a very good marriage. Keep that in mind.'

'You have to be joking,' she muttered tightly.

'I realise that the martyr mentality has got a good grip on you. But I'm asking you to give us a chance.'

Her bewildered eyes flickered over his taut features. She marked the fierce determination etched there, recognised the suppressed emotion edging his dark drawl. His tension sprang out at her, as though he felt he was putting his pride on the line in making such a request. It shook her, unsettled her on some level she was reluctant to probe. Hurriedly she turned away in silence.

'Leah, do you want the information I have on Woods?'

Her stomach heaved. Dear God but Nik was unscrupulous. How on earth had he contrived to find out so much about Paul late last night? But then money talked, didn't it? And the few facts might have been correct but the rest was lies. Lies it suited Nik to tell, and cheap at the price if they undermined her faith in the man she loved. But Nik did not know how strong that love was. How could he? Love didn't enter into his requirements for marriage or his extra-marital activities.

How could he even begin to understand what it had been like for her to emerge from the emotional desert of her loneliness, her sense of inadequacy? Paul was interested in her. He listened to her, encouraged her, supported her. He *cared* about her in a way a man like Nik Andreakis could never care. She would not let that go, she swore to herself, not her one chance in life to love and be loved.

Nik could find a dozen women to satisfy his wifely requirements. Looks, physical appeal, the ability to be a good hostess and no doubt a commensurate ability to turn a blind eye when her husband strayed into other beds—just one of those *male* things, you know, something no mere woman could possibly understand! Well, the tolerant wife wouldn't be Leah! She had no doubt at all that he would be flooded by a rush of eager applicants, ninety per cent of whom would be far more prepared for the downside of being married to Nik Andreakis than Leah had been at a naïve seventeen!

A migraine headache attacked when she was on the flight back to London. She stumbled sickly through the airport, fell into the waiting limousine and practically crawled into the house. Upstairs in her beautiful bedroom suite, her maid took one look at her pain-racked, perspiring face and rushed to close the curtains and help her down on to the bed. When she was alone, she cried, tears seeping down silently from her lowered eyelids, dripping on to the pillow. She was beyond thought, beyond anything but simple reaction.

The next morning her strength returned and, along with it, her determination. She made plans and acted on them. The only piece of jewellery she possessed which was truly hers had belonged to her maternal grandmother. It was a cobweb-fine diamond necklace and she was extremely attached to it. But it was her only passport to freedom. She had to have cash to live on until she found her feet. And it might be news to Nik, she reflected bitterly, but she was well aware that it would be very tough for her to find those feet.

When she walked out of Nik's house, she wasn't taking any of the trappings of the old life with her. No credit cards, no fancy clothes, no jewellery. She intended to make it on her own. She had no right to his money or his financial support. After all, she had never been his wife. And why should she go for a divorce when she could seek an annulment? Her marriage had been born out of blackmail, out of murky secrets and duress. Its dissolution would be as plain and honest as Leah could make it.

She sold her grandmother's necklace in a jewellers. It hurt, it filled her with guilt but she hoped that if the mother she barely remembered was looking down she would understand her daughter's desperation.

Back at the house, she started to clear out her wardrobes in search of plainer, more casual clothes—jeans, T-shirts, sweaters, skirts. She would go to a small hotel until she could find cheaper accommodation. And then she was going to find a job, any job...it didn't matter how menial. As helpless as a newborn baby? No way!

The internal phone rang. It was Petros, informing her that she had a visitor downstairs. A Mr Woods. Paul had actually come to the house? Leah was shaken. When he hadn't phoned last night she had assumed he was out, and had intended to ring him later when she had finally accomplished her removal from Nik's house.

Paul was standing in the drawing-room, studying a Picasso drawing, Nik's one artistic weakness.

'You shouldn't have come here!'

'Is it real?' He indicated the drawing.

'Yes.' She had so much to tell him, she didn't know where to start, didn't know what she should tell, what she should keep to herself. There was, she discovered in confusion, an odd vein of loyalty to Nik somewhere inside her. She didn't like to see Paul in Nik's house. It just didn't seem *right*. And maybe that was why she didn't feel she could throw herself into Paul's arms.

'I was told you weren't home when I tried to phone you last night,' He revealed, tight-mouthed.

'But I was.' Was Nik responsible for that development? Were even her calls to be screened and censored now? But then she reminded herself that it didn't matter any more. She was leaving. 'I've told Nik I want a divorce,' she imparted tautly. 'And I'm moving out today.'

Paul's handsome face split into a wide grin. He crossed the carpet in one stride and grabbed her. 'Darling, that's fantastic!'

As he attempted to kiss her, Leah angled her head back out of reach, her nervous tension rocketing. 'Not *here* . . . it doesn't feel right,' she muttered shakily.

Paul laughed. 'I hope it feels better in my apartment tonight.' He kept his arms linked round her.

'Paul . . .' Leah swallowed hard. 'I'm not moving in with you.'

He frowned and then his brow cleared. 'It might count against you in the divorce . . . you're right. Sensible girl. After the hell *he's* put you through, why should you pose as the guilty partner? It might affect your settlement.'

'I don't want Nik's money.'

Paul's bright blue eyes narrowed. 'Don't be silly, Leah. I know you already have your father's inheritance but——'

Leah tensed. Why was all the talk about money? 'A history of chasing wealthy women' . . . Nik's jibe returned to her. Angrily she thrust it away. 'We'll have to talk about that.'

'I'm only thinking about you. You're not used to roughing it. I couldn't bear to feel I was dragging you down.'

'You wouldn't be. I'll be free and we'll be just like any other couple,' she reasoned in a rush. 'You should go now. You shouldn't be here...'

'Relax, for God's sake.' Paul was wandering round the room, taking careful account of the antique furniture and scrutinising the remainder of the pictures. 'How much of this stuff is yours?' he enquired, with a low whistle of admiration.

Leah heard the tone of suppressed excitement, saw the avaricious look in his face and something died inside her. All Paul seemed able to think about was what she would bring with her.

Her deadened eyes fell on her mother's elegant little writing desk, passed on to her by her father after her wedding, the only piece of furniture in the entire house which belonged to her. Something buzzed at the back of her mind as she looked at it but she was too upset by what she had just seen in Paul to be able to concentrate.

'None of it's mine. In fact, I signed a pre-nuptial agreement before my marriage and I don't get anything,' she lied shakily. 'And the problem in Paris with my father's estate? I'm afraid that money has to go towards settling his debts...'

'Debts?' Paul gaped at her. 'You're having me on.'

'No; when I walk out of this house I'll be penniless.'

'But you never told me that!' he condemned, and then fell suddenly silent. His mouth compressed. 'You shouldn't move out without giving it very careful thought. God knows, I'm only thinking of what's best for you——'

'Of course,' she managed.

'I would feel really bad if you gave all this up purely for my benefit.' His smooth insincerity twisted her stomach. 'I mean, suppose it didn't work out between us? I have to be honest. I'm not sure I could handle that responsibility. We both need to think very carefully about what we're doing.'

He said he had an appointment. He wanted to extract himself without embarrassment and mull over what she had told him. Leah felt like an automaton, was scared to *feel* again. You fool, you fool, echoed at the back of her head. She had fallen for the first smoothie to pay her attention. And of course Paul had listened, supported, encouraged. He had flattered her battered pride, buttered her up with compliments. Naturally. He had wanted her to leave Nik but only if she brought Nik's money with her.

She went back upstairs and worked frantically to complete her packing. Nothing had changed, she told herself. Paul might no longer figure in her future but she didn't want Nik there either. She was finished with Nik, finished with the past. And she damned well didn't need any man to lean on! Three in a row. Her father, Nik, Paul. All of them using, manipulating, abusing. And what had she done? She had put up as much resistance as a boneless, brainless rag doll! Her anger was so great, she could hardly contain it.

Her cases downstairs, she called a cab. Boyce hovered.

'I won't be needing you,' she said, and when he argued added, 'I'm leaving him.'

Boyce looked shattered. But everybody would know soon enough, she reasoned.

The cab came. As it drove off she took a last look back at the house and it was scary knowing that she was leaving security behind. The cab driver was very helpful about suggesting a hotel. She checked in and went out immediately to buy a newspaper. Finding somewhere to stay and a job were her only priorities.

A knock on the door of her room sounded at ten that night. Leah slid off the bed and unlocked the door. She took one devastated look at Nik and attempted to shut it again. His golden features taut and furious, he planted a hand against the door and thrust it back to the wall, forcing her to retreat.

'How the hell did you know where I was?'

'Boyce had the wit to follow you.' Nik leant back against the door and locked it.

'He had no right to do that,' she said bitterly.

'He works for me and you're a prime target for kidnapping. He did what he had to do,' Nik bit out. 'Just as I'm about to do what I have to do.'

Leah stiffened, clashing with murderous black eyes. 'And what's that supposed to mean?'

'I'm not letting you go,' he breathed fiercely.

Pain slivered through her but her sapphire eyes gleamed with contempt. 'You're like a dog with a bone you buried and forgot about. You had no interest in that bone until somebody else dug it up!'

'You are my wife.'

'Since when? Since when was I your wife? You think *feeding* and *clothing* covers it?' Leah jibed helplessly. 'Well, you can keep your clothing and your food and your rotten money because I don't want any of it. Any more than I want you!'

'You always wanted me . . .'

'You missed the boat. I got over you a long time ago,' Leah flung with a sort of embittered enjoyment that was new to her.

'But you still want me to pay,' Nik slotted in, strolling fluidly closer. Shimmering dark eyes assailed hers with force, the anger he was controlling blatant in that hard stare. 'So you walk out without even telling me. I didn't even qualify for a note——'

'And what did you expect? Dear Nik, it's been a lousy five years, goodbye? That's about all I could have to say to you!'

'You brought him into my house,' Nik murmured roughly.

Leah stilled, her hectic colour sliding away, utterly silenced by the news that he was aware of Paul's visit.

'And no doubt if it had suited you you would have taken him to our bed as well!'

An edged laugh was torn from Leah. The smouldering tension in the atmosphere was so thick she could taste it but she refused to be intimidated. This confrontation was long overdue. And finally she was having her say. '*We* never had a bed, so fulfilling that ambition would have been a little difficult!'

'Stop it,' Nik grated, a tiny muscle pulling at the corner of his compressed mouth. 'I am trying not to lose my temper.'

'I don't want you and your temper in this room. I want you to leave——'

'Not without you.'

'Why? What's so special about me?' Leah demanded tempestuously, out of control as she had never been before, her stormy emotions feasting on every acid word. 'Why don't you marry one of your bimbos, Nik? Or am I missing something here? Were the bimbos as much of a front as our marriage was? You see, I am not as dumb as I used to be. Why do you want me to stay so badly? Could it be that you're gay?'

The instant she said it she regretted it. She hadn't meant to go that far in her need to lash out. A shudder ran through Nik, naked outrage flashing across his savagely handsome features.

'No...not gay,' he bit out with considerable effort. As he spoke, he shrugged off his jacket and ripped at his tie. 'Maybe you need a demonstration...'

Leah blinked, her blinding surge of rage having more or less vented itself on that final accusation which she was guiltily aware had, for Nik, been the ultimate insult. 'What are you doing?'

'Something I should have done years ago.' He tore his shirt out of his beautifully tailored trousers and pulled it over his dark head, discarding it in a heap with the rest.

'Would you please put your clothes back on?' Leah said unsteadily, and she knew she sounded ridiculous, which didn't help.

'Scared you'd see something you might like? *Cristo...*' Nik intoned rawly. 'To think I was about to waste time courting my wife! To think I was going to do bloody stupid things like buying you flowers and taking you out! Get on that bed...'

'Have you gone crazy?' Leah gasped in disbelief.

Before she could move, Nik caught her up in his powerful arms and dumped her down on the divan behind her. He came down on top of her so fast that she hadn't a hope of evading him. Waves of shock coursed through her.

'You're my wife,' Nik growled down at her, as if that were sufficient justification.

'Let go of me...you're flattening me!' Leah slung back at him in fury.

'Maybe you'll get to like it.' Nik shifted sinuously above her and meshed one hand into her tumbled hair. He stared down at her for a long, timeless moment. '*Theos*, I am so hungry for you, I ache,' he muttered raggedly.

Leah's entire body was an angry pillow of rejection. 'Go find a bimbo, Nik,' she urged shakily. 'At least you won't have to tell *her* lies.'

'I'm not lying. How could I? A man's body betrays his arousal.' Sliding a lean thigh between hers, Nik moved against her, shamelessly introducing her to the hard bulge of his manhood. 'No lie,' he completed huskily.

Pink starred her cheeks even as an insidious heat flared between her thighs. 'You're disgusting.'

'I want you.' He buried his mouth hotly in a hollow just below her collarbone.

'No!' she whispered frantically, feeling that hot wire of sensation pull tight and reacting in panic.

He lifted his dark head, a blaze of desire in his hot gaze, and then he took her mouth with explosive passion. It was an act of possession, a stamp of ownership blatant in its intent to dominate. And she knew it, fought what he was making her feel with every fibre, but with every kiss, with every sweetly invasive thrust of his tongue, he taught her to want the next. Her hands rose, curved compulsively to the satin-smooth skin of his shoulders, holding him to her.

He rolled over, carrying her with him, and dispensed with her T-shirt by whipping it over her head. He uttered a savage groan as her unbound breasts rubbed against his hair-roughened chest and a split-second later she was lying flat again, his hands shaping the pouting mounds he had discovered.

She shut her eyes, gasping for breath, all reasoning power wrested from her. He found a distended pink nipple with his mouth and she dug her hips into the mattress, her back arching, a wildness she had never known tearing at her. Her heart was racing, her skin damp, every cell firing on red alert. He employed his tongue and his teeth in a grazing torment of a caress, cupping her breasts, sucking at the sensitive buds he had aroused. And she speared her fingers into the depths of his thick, silky hair and moaned with the intensity of the pleasure.

'You are mine,' Nik grated in a voice so tortured that she didn't initially realise that he had spoken in English.

She wasn't listening anyway. He was apart from her. She didn't like it. She lifted her head and touched his sensual mouth with her lips and then, more daringly, with the tip of her tongue, unconsciously imitating what she had learnt from him. He shuddered and accepted the invitation with a raw passion that consumed her, his arms banding so tightly around her that she could barely breathe.

They rolled over again, welded together by an increasingly uncontrollable excitement. She heard something rip. It meant nothing to her. She was lost entirely in the heat and the scent and the feel of him. He felt so hot. His scent was an aphrodisiac that sent her senses spinning. Every tiny shift of his lean, muscular body against hers drove her wild, every caress an incitement to a hunger fast reaching fever pitch.

Her breasts had become incredibly sensitive and he played with the tender flesh with every atom of erotic expertise in his repertoire. His fingers flirted with the damp tangle of curls at the base of her taut stomach and she panted for oxygen and then moaned helplessly as his heated exploration roved to the very heart of her.

She couldn't be still, couldn't control her own limbs. The wild pulsebeat of desire had taken her over. Her hips jerked up in a rhythm she didn't know but somehow found, her head thrown back, her slender throat extended. An intolerable ache was building up, making her sob out his name over and over again.

Nik said something in Greek and groaned against her reddened mouth like a man in torment. 'I can't wait.'

And then he was there where she most wanted him to be, pushing up her thighs with wildly impatient hands, sliding against the honeyed welcome he had prepared for himself. Her eyes flew wide, passion-glazed sapphire locking with burning jet. She tensed. She could feel him, hot and smooth and hard, suddenly threateningly male. She searched his taut features and saw such a look of vulnerability momentarily etched in those beautiful eyes that her heart lurched. And all of a sudden she wanted him so badly it hurt.

He entered her with a stifled groan, slowly, gently, and the pain she was braced to withstand was merely a fleeting stab of discomfort, quickly past and forgotten under the storm of fiery sensation which engulfed her. Instant meltdown. Every thrust lifted her higher, burning out everything but the feeling, submerging her in the hungry demand of her own need. He moved faster and she wrapped her arms round him, out of control, her heart pounding, her pulses racing, and then it happened, an explosion of white-hot heat flying up inside her, sending her out of her mind with its strength.

'*S'agapo...s'agapo.*' Nik drove into her violently and then shuddered with the force of his own release.

Blissfully pliant, still floating gloriously slowly back to earth, Leah snuggled into him as he slid onto his side, every quivering curve glued to him. She pressed her lips to a muscular brown shoulder, nostrils flaring at the musky damp scent of him. The light went out. Silence fell. Leah wandered over the edge of complete exhaustion into sleep, sprawled on top of him.

CHAPTER FIVE

NIK'S voice, talking Greek ... but she was in *bed*. Her
feathery lashes shot up, revealing startled sapphire-blue
eyes. Her arrested attention fell on Nik. He had his back
turned to her. He was standing at the window, one lean
hand occupied by a mobile phone. Shock rolled over her
in a debilitating wave. A Technicolor replay of the events
of the night before sizzled through her brain, not a single
X-rated second deleted.

And she couldn't explain how it had happened. That
was the most appalling discovery of all. One minute she
had been screaming at him in fury, the next ...? As she
stiffened below the crumpled sheet, unfamiliar muscles
complained and a faint ache intimately reminded her of
the explosive passion which had flared up between them.

Hot colour burnished her cheeks. Had Nik not still
been physically present, she would have believed it was
all a dream ... a nightmare, she amended with a shudder.
She rubbed at her temples, vaguely conscious that her
head was sore, her throat slightly raw.

Join the bimbo fraternity, she told herself with sudden
fury. But join at the bottom of the class.

The average bimbo had a certain native cunning, knew
where she was going and how. Leah had fallen at the
first major hurdle. She had finally got up the courage
to leave Nik, had felt good about that decision, indeed
had felt empowered by it ... and then he had brought
her down on this bed and kissed her and inexplicably
the balance of power had swung violently back to the
enemy; for he was the enemy. Anyone capable of re-

ducing her to this level was definitely the enemy. As she moved her head on the pillow, it swam.

Her tortured gaze rested on him, on the angle of his well-shaped dark head, the breadth of his shoulders beneath the fine cloth of his jacket, the jut of his narrow hips as he dug a lean hand into the pocket of his tailored trousers and splayed his long legs. And she was shattered by just how much she *liked* looking at him, how familiar every gesture was, every fluid change of stance. Pain traversed her tight features. She knew then how it had happened.

She had blocked out Nik's attraction, blocked out the hunger, blocked out every thought of him. Self-preservation had taught her to do that. But all along that attraction had still been there, a sexual craving denied and buried and made all the more dangerous by that suppression. It was that same craving which had escaped and betrayed her in Nik's arms. Given the opportunity, she had grabbed him . . . just as he had always said she would.

Hot moisture lashed the back of her eyelids but she wouldn't let the tears fall. She really didn't feel well but that was no good reason to give way to such weakness.

Nik turned and strolled across to the bed. He was too much of a predator not to smile, his sensual mouth curving with self-satisfaction as he looked down at her. He couldn't even hide it. He settled down on the edge of the mattress, lustrous dark eyes tracking over her intently. 'It's a beautiful morning.'

She could hear the wind lashing the rain against the windows.

'In Athens,' he added softly, lifting a hand and skating a finger along the taut line of her lower lip. 'And if you tell me you're not coming—— No, don't you dare tell me that,' he warned as her lips began to part. 'Not after last night.'

'That was just sex,' Leah bit out, a heady flush staining her skin.

His smile merely grew in brilliance as he lowered his dark head. 'Never *just* sex,' he reproved huskily. 'Fabulous, wonderful, incredible sex. If the jet wasn't on stand-by, I'd still be in bed.'

Her teeth gritted. 'Yesterday, I left you——'

'*Theos mou*! And today we are closer than we have ever been. Life is so unpredictable,' Nik pointed out with immovable self-assurance. 'Think of this as the first day of our marriage.'

'That is the most nauseating suggestion I've ever heard!' Leah snapped, goaded beyond bearing. 'I don't want to go to Athens.'

Nik slid upright. 'But you will. My family are all gathering to meet you at my mother's home. I don't care if I have to drag you kicking and screaming all the way to the airport,' he delivered with sudden harshness, his strong jawline clenching. 'To be blunt, *agape mou*, you made your decision last night!'

'You did it deliberately!' Leah gasped.

'Yes.' The unvarnished affirmative was like a slap in the face. 'Now why don't you get dressed? I instructed your maid to pack for you. I assume that what you have here wasn't planned with Greece in mind.'

Wrapping herself awkwardly in the sheet under Nik's grimly amused gaze, Leah was conscious of her swimming head and for the first time acknowledged that she really wasn't feeling well at all.

She went into the bathroom. This was her penance, that was what it was. Her punishment for stupidity. The knowledge that she had helplessly connived in her own downfall was a bitter pill to swallow. But Leah made herself swallow it, trailing out every thought, every feeling with masochistic candour.

She had believed she was in love with Paul. Had Paul been her escape route from her marriage? Deep down had she needed the belief that someone loved her to work up the courage to leave Nik? The idea that she was loved had given her strength, had restored her faith in herself. But yesterday she had been forced to face reality.

Paul hadn't loved her...but had *she* loved *him*? For a while he had made her feel good about herself. But yesterday she had seen through his superficial charm so clearly that she had marvelled that she had ever been taken in. Yes, it had been very painful, having to accept that he had viewed her as a purely profitable enterprise. But did she still long for him? No, there had been a terrible finality to the sense of alienation she had felt. She never wanted to see Paul again. So had she ever loved him? Or had it been an infatuation born of her loneliness?

Lord, the bathroom was hot. Leah sank down dizzily on the side of the bath in the midst of trying to dress herself. She felt as weak as a kitten and light-headed. It was becoming an immense challenge to concentrate but still she forced herself to the task.

Last night had been a ghastly mistake. Did she now hang her head in shame and let Nik browbeat her into staying with him even though she felt that that was the very worst thing she could do? She lifted an unsteady hand to her pounding temples and knew she had to make herself strong, knew she had to stand up for herself.

Emerging from the bathroom, she leant back against the door-frame for support. Nik surveyed her with narrowed eyes. 'What's wrong?'

'I think I've got the flu...but that's not important.' Breathing in to sustain herself, she stared sickly back at him. 'I'm staying here...not coming back to you——'

'You're not feeling well. You don't know what you're saying,' Nik cut in. 'I'll take you down to the car.'

'No!' she gasped, tears of frustration and weakness gathering in her eyes as her wobbling lower limbs threatened to collapse under her. 'Don't you ever listen? You're wrong for me!'

Nik swept her up in his arms in spite of her feeble attempt to evade him.

'*Please*!' Her failure to get through to him or persuade him to put her down again drove her crazy. 'I don't want to go with you. I want to stay here.'

'*Theos*...you're expecting *him*, aren't you?' he raked down at her with barely restrained anger. 'If you weren't sick I'd shake you!'

Her cases were already gone, she saw in horror as Nik thrust open the door of her room, holding her steady with one powerful arm.

'Let me go!' Her swimming head fell back against his shoulder as he strode down the corridor.

'If I let you go you'll fall in a heap at my feet.' He muttered something guttural in Greek, his set, dark features as unyielding as stone as he hit the call button for the lift again with positive violence.

'I want a divorce...I'm not going to Greece!' she gasped strickenly.

'You should have thought of that last night.' He stepped into the lift.

'It was a *mistake*!' she protested, unable even to lift her pounding head. 'Put me down...'

'You don't know what you're doing or saying,' Nik contended with tenacious determination, refusing even to meet her distressed gaze.

'I know...' She would have screamed the assurance had she had the strength. As it was, the amount of energy she had expended on frantic argument and the stress of her own emotional conflict had absolutely drained her. Nick's strong, dark features blurred as her weighted eyelids lowered. 'I hate you,' she mumbled hoarsely.

She drifted in and out of awareness from that point, too utterly wretched to consider anything but her own physical misery. Nik carried her on to the jet, wrapped in a blanket, and a while later she surfaced to hear a vaguely familiar voice sigh, 'The poor thing. I feel so sorry for her,' with a kind of oozing insincerity that grated on her hearing.

She recognised the stewardess, sultry wine-tinted mouth to the fore as she passed Nik a glass. As Nik lifted Leah and tilted the contents of the glass to her mouth, she said, 'She hopes it's fatal.'

'Drink; it'll make you feel better,' Nik urged.

Nothing would. Bitterness enveloped Leah. Nik had taken cruel advantage of her illness. Was nothing sacrosanct? As another shiver racked her aching body and she drank the noxious liquid because she knew that argument was futile, she looked up at him with condemning sapphire eyes. An act which ran little short of kidnapping was inexcusable.

'I couldn't leave you alone in a hotel in this condition,' Nik murmured as if she had spoken out loud.

'I'll never forgive you,' Leah mumbled. 'I hope you catch it!'

Unexpectedly he laughed, the arm cradled round her shoulders curving her close in a blatant challenging of contagion which didn't surprise her. Nik was never ill. The very idea amused him. He had a godlike faith in his own robust health.

Her impressions became increasingly more fleeting from that point on. She lost her sense of time, her ability to distinguish between waking and sleeping. Had she been sleeping? she wondered when her eyes took in the crowds milling around them. A fleeting exchange of Greek told her that they must have landed. It was the airport, she decided bitterly, and shut her eyes again, engulfed by a drowning sense of failure.

A sharp exchange of voices dragged her back to awareness. She was laid down on something, the blanket removed, a thermometer thrust into her dry mouth. Her heavy eyelids lifted on a white ceiling. Not an airport, a hospital, she decided. She could hear Nik talking. He sounded angry, upset, and the other voice, which had been equally angry, was suddenly soft, soothing... a richly expressive, very female voice. With an enormous effort, Leah turned her head to one side.

A woman in a white coat stood in the circle of Nik's arms. With one slim hand she was smoothing his black hair, caressing his hard jawline, and even as Leah looked she was reaching up to kiss him. Her lashes dropped again in shock.

The thermometer was removed... soon afterwards, a long time afterwards? She was sliding in and out of awareness. The next time she opened her eyes the woman was giving something to Nik and she saw her properly— the superb oval of her classically beautiful face below her crown of glossy black hair, the creamy skin and the great dark eyes brimming with so much warmth as they rested on Nik. A dry cough jolted through Leah and both heads spun round.

Nik moved first. 'I thought you were asleep. This is Dr Kiriakos——'

'Eleni,' his companion inserted with an air of rather forced informality as she regarded Leah with cool, professional distance. 'I am afraid that you will feel worse before you feel better, Leah.'

Leah closed her eyes, shutting them out in self-defence. She already felt a hundred times worse. She could feel her crumpled clothes, shiny, perspiring face and limp, damp hair. Her very bones were hurting. She wanted to cry but she didn't have the energy. Dear God, he brought me to his mistress for treatment; only Nik could be that cruel. Never in her life had Leah felt more savaged.

'I was really scared,' Nik muttered roughly as he carried her somewhere. 'You looked so ill. I thought it might be pneumonia or something. And I didn't know what to do and I panicked.'

Panicked? Nik? It was an unlikely image in Leah's disorientated mind. Then he was talking to someone in Greek, yet another female, this one younger, warmer, less controlled. Leah was dimly aware of what sounded like a pretty heated argument and then she drifted off again, too wretched to care what was happening to her or around her.

There was a rushing sound somewhere in the background. Leah's memory banks produced a jumbled mass of images and feelings. She had had a fever. She had gone from perspiring, shivering misery into the heat of what had felt like hell, with a whirling Catherine wheel of pain behind her temples. Day and night had merged indistinguishably.

She remembered being sponged down repeatedly and being so weak that even speaking was beyond her. And she remembered Nik, silhouetted against the lamplit darkness of an unfamiliar room, Nik, hunched in a seat, oddly grey-looking in the dawn light. There had been other people too but it felt like too much effort to remember them.

Her eyes opened. A maid was drawing curtains back on a spectacular wall of glass through which Leah could see a slice of cloudless, densely blue sky. Then the sunlight blinded her and she turned her head away, gratefully recognising that her throat didn't hurt, her head didn't ache and her muscles no longer protested against every movement. The door closed. A sudden pressing need for the bathroom assailed her.

She attempted to sit up. Her body was disobedient. With a moan of impatience she rolled her legs off the edge of the divan and slid down in an ungraceful heap on to the mercifully thick, deep pile of the carpet. It was a vast room. Lamplight had confusingly shrunk its contours.

Using the bed as a brace, she pushed herself upright and swayed like a drunk, registering that she was not quite as recovered as she had fondly imagined. But obstinacy got her to the *en suite*.

An accidental meeting with her own reflection in a mirror horrified her. Who was that white scarecrow with the lank hank of hair? Fighting her own weakness, she knelt beside the bath to turn on the taps. At least if she was clean she would feel better.

'*Cristo*! What the hell do you think you are doing?'

Leah flinched and clutched the side of the bath. Nik towered over her, intimidatingly tall and dark. He looked tremendously elegant in a fabulously well-cut cream suit which merely accentuated his exotic colouring.

'Are you crazy?' he thundered, not content with having frightened her half out of her wits. 'You should be in bed!'

'I want a bath.' Leah rested her cheek dully down on the cold ceramic edge, weak as a kitten. And then it came to her... Like a slow-motion replay from some distant dream, she saw him with Eleni Kiriakos again. Her heart seemed to stop beating. A chill like an icy winter wind enclosed her shrinking flesh.

'A bath when you can't even stand up?' Nik derided as he bent down to lift her.

Leah burst into floods of tears, disconcerting him as much as herself. But she had had no warning, no chance to stem those tears. They simply gushed forth as though someone had thrown an overload switch and forced their release. And the effect on Nik was little short of staggering.

With a stifled imprecation in Greek, he scooped her up and cradled her while he apologised profusely for upsetting her and assured her that of course she could have a bath if she wanted one *that* badly. It was just that she had been so ill, he stressed, and he was naturally afraid that she would over-exert herself and suffer a relapse. It was Nik metaphorically on his knees, Nik as she had never known him.

Ten minutes later, Leah slid into her bath, and had not the image of the beautiful doctor still been lingering she might almost have been touched by the amount of concern Nik was displaying. As it was, she simply didn't understand and was still too weak to devote her low energy resources to the vexing question of why Nik should have gone to such lengths to force her to come to Greece to put a front on a marriage that had never been anything other than a charade for both of them.

Washing her hair exhausted her. When she emerged from the bathroom, she made no objection to being carried back to bed by Nik, although she was amazed that he had waited with such patience for her.

'I can hear the sea,' she murmured, finally identifying that rushing sound as waves surging up on to a shore.

'Do you remember anything of the trip here?' Unreadable dark eyes rested on her.

'Nothing,' she sighed.

'We're not in Athens. When you were ill, there was little point in taking you to my mother's home. So I brought you here instead.'

'And where is here?'

'Thrathos, a small island which my father purchased shortly before his death. The perfect place for you to recuperate,' Nik said smoothly.

'An island?' Leah raised an uncertain hand to her damp brow, her physical weakness slowing up her ability to think, but the one thought that did cross her dazed mind was that she knew precious little about her husband of five years.

A smiling, dark-eyed maid provided an interruption by arriving with a breakfast tray. Leah's empty stomach gave a tiny leap as she registered just how hungry she was. 'How long have I been here?' she asked.

'Two days——'

'*Two*?'

A flying knock sounded on the door and a teenager in cerise cycle shorts and a cropped top, her long hair a mass of glossy black ringlets, erupted into the room with a wide grin. 'Great, you're feeling better...'

'Leah, this is my niece, Apollonia——'

'Everyone calls me Ponia,' the tiny brunette broke in cheerfully. 'I came to meet you at the airport but you won't remember me. You were practically unconscious.'

'I remember your voice.' Leah smiled. Ponia's friendliness was infectious. Yet once again she suffered that feeling of almost embarrassing ignorance. Nik's niece. He could have a dozen for all she knew.

'Leah has to rest, not be talked into a relapse,' Nik warned.

Ponia reddened, obviously sensitive to any reference to her chatterbox tendencies.

'But I'd love to have some company.' Leah shot Nik's hard profile a speaking glance of reproach.

'Terrif!' Ponia plonked herself down casually on the foot of the bed. 'You know, I thought you'd be older—but then maybe you're older than you look! What age are you?'

'Ponia...' Nik breathed.

'Twenty-two——'

'You got married at *seventeen*?' Ponia swivelled her eyes, whose expression was a combination of shock and fascination, across to her uncle. 'And you agreed with my parents that you think that is far too young for me to be seriously dating?' she demanded.

Registering the gathering storm in Nik's discomfited features and holding back her own sudden desire to laugh, Leah found herself surging to the ebullient teenager's rescue. 'You speak marvellous English, Ponia.'

'I go to school in England. I wish I'd known what age you were,' she complained afresh. 'I would have visited

and got to know you *years* ago...in spite of what
everybody else said!'

Nik released his breath in a sudden hiss and addressed
his niece in Greek. Ponia stiffened, a mutinous expression tightening her pretty face as she bent her head.
What had the Andreakis family said about Nik's wife
whom they had never met? Leah could not help being
curious.

'Don't let her tire you out,' Nik sighed, heading for
the door.

'Men are really *thick* sometimes,' Ponia muttered and
then threw a comically dismayed look at Leah.

'Aren't they just!' Leah laughed, belatedly realising
how very depressed she had been feeling before Ponia's
arrival. It was the flu which had done that to her, she
told herself.

'I had to twist his arm to get to come here with you,'
Ponia confided. 'Nik always feels sorry for me because
I have such a drag of a time when I'm home between
terms.'

'I suppose all your friends are in England,' Leah said.

'Oh, it's not that, it's the family being so *old*.' Ponia
grimaced. 'They're all living in the last century!'

'Your parents?' Leah was trying not to smile.

'Well, they're the youngest, I guess,' the teenager conceded grudgingly. 'Only early fifties——'

'The youngest? Nik's only thirty...your mother, his
sister, is that much older?'

'And her two sisters are older again. My grandmother
is well into her seventies.'

Nik must have been a very late baby. Leah found
herself having to rearrange her assumptions. For some
reason she had assumed that Nik was the eldest child,
not the youngest. It was rather unusual to have a
gap of over twenty years between children, she
thought absently.

'If only I'd known what you were like sooner,' Ponia was still lamenting. 'I was so madly curious about you, too.'

'Is that why you came to meet us at the airport?' Leah smiled again.

'No, that was because I wanted you to know how welcome you were. I think the way my family have treated you is horrible,' Ponia said very earnestly.

Leah sipped at her coffee. 'I——'

'And you were the exact same age as I am now,' the teenager continued heatedly as she sprang off the bed and wandered over to the window. 'I know how I would feel if my husband's family refused to have anything to do with me... I'd be very hurt and then I'd get furious!'

Illumination sank in on Leah. The Andreakis family had evidently rejected her sight unseen. Nik had not deliberately excluded her from his family circle. But Leah felt neither hurt nor furious. Theirs had not been a normal marriage. She had had more to worry about than the uninterest of Nik's distant family...although she was suddenly distinctly grateful *not* to be a guest in her mother-in-law's house.

'I'm not furious,' she said wryly.

'But it was so unfair. It wasn't your fault that Nik fell madly in love with you and backed out of his betrothal with Eleni Kiriakos!' Ponia grimaced impressively in the pin-dropping silence. 'I mean, that was just one of those things and it would have been a lot worse if he'd fallen for you *after* he'd married her... don't you think?'

But mercifully Leah was saved from the necessity of a reply as a maid entered and addressed Ponia.

'Rats! Mother on the phone,' the teenager groaned, and then grinned. 'She won't ask any questions, I bet, but she has to be just gasping to know all about you! She's terribly fond of Nik...' She frowned, noticing Leah's waxen pallor for the first time. 'You should get some sleep. You look really drained. I'll see you later.'

'Lovely,' Leah said shakily, flying on automatic pilot after a revelation which had literally depth-charged her out of her weak languor. She tasted blood in her mouth, registered that she had bitten down painfully on her tongue to prevent a shocked exclamation escaping her. Well, well, well, she thought, struggling manfully to recover from the shock.

CHAPTER SIX

ELENI and Nik. Nik and Eleni. Leah was shattered. Five years ago they had been engaged to be married. Evidently Nik might not have been averse to a little Parisian flirtation but he had already had his future wife lined up. At least he had, Leah adjusted, until her father had intervened to demand a change of bride. Leah felt really sick as the full meaning of what she had learnt sank in.

Nik and Eleni Kiriakos were lovers. So why had Nik insisted that Leah remain his wife? Why had he refused to snatch at his freedom? Didn't he want to marry Eleni? Or was he quite content to retain the good doctor as his mistress, his patently devoted mistress, who couldn't even keep her paws off him in the presence of his wife?

Leah shuddered; she presumed that there was nothing in the Hippocratic oath that forbade such behaviour. No wonder Nik had been so bitter about their marriage! But Nik had not chosen to tell her the whole truth of what their marriage had cost him.

On the other hand, Nik was certainly beginning to settle the score for what he had suffered. Could that possibly be mere coincidence? Dear God, Nik *had* to hate her! It was a nonsense surely for him to say that he did not?

More wretched, more isolated than she had ever felt in her life before, Leah buried her aching head in the pillows. Just as Max Harrington had manipulated Nik and forcibly rearranged his life five years ago, Nik was now bringing to bear a similar pressure on Max's daughter.

Nik had first revealed what might have been called a 'sudden' attraction towards his hitherto invisible wife the day Leah had told him she was in love with another man. Previous to that, he had believed that she still loved him and no doubt over the years he had reaped a vicarious satisfaction from punishing her for her father's sins by demonstrating his complete indifference towards her.

He didn't yet know that Paul was out of her life. But he had been ruthlessly determined to achieve that end. Why? An eye for an eye, a tooth for a tooth? Nik had been deprived of Eleni five years ago. Was he intent on putting Leah through the same torment of losing a loved one? Was he capable of being that sadistic? Her father was out of reach, had been out of reach of any form of retribution even while alive by virtue of his blackmail, but Leah was very much within reach and always had been.

Yes, Nik could be sadistic. She remembered his cruel assurance that even Max couldn't force him to perform like a stud in her bed. Her pounding head was whirling. She thought back shrinkingly to Nik's passionate possession of her, only now recalled his unashamed admission that that had been a deliberate ploy. At the time she had believed that he meant he had slept with her both to reinforce his contention that they *could* have a real marriage and to tear a gaping hole in her confident assertion that she loved Paul . . . even to punish her for daring to defy him.

Only now did she see another, even more humiliating explanation for that night. A turn of the screw, a heightening of the victim's torment . . . Nik, with all his considerable sexual *savoir-faire*, setting out with cool calculation to seduce his wife and thus throw her into absolute turmoil. Suddenly she felt painfully degraded by her own weakness in his arms, the unsuspected vulnerability which had made her a pushover for all that smouldering, sizzling Greek machismo. And Nik had just *loved* that discovery. The awareness was like a knife twisting in an open wound.

Exhaustion sent her into an uneasy sleep from which she awoke to find that it was after midnight. She had slept solid for more than twelve hours. But evidently it had done her good. Physically she was feeling much stronger...even if she did feel as though she was on the brink of starvation.

Pulling on a light robe, she went off in search of food. Her mind was awash with all the frightening thoughts she had endured earlier and, preoccupied as she was, she got the shock of her life when Nik appeared silently in a doorway just as she was passing.

A hiss of unformed sound erupted from her lips and she backed away in haste, her shoulder-blades colliding with the cold stone wall on the other side of the passageway.

'Looking for a phone, *pethi mou*?'

In the dim light, his striking features might have been a bronze sculpture, eyes a mere sliver of black below the dark crescents of his lashes.

Leah pressed a helpless hand to the crazed thump of her heartbeat. 'A ph—phone...?' she stammered blankly.

'Judging by the length of your calls to Woods, you were heavily into the substitute of telephone sex,' Nik murmured with silken insolence. 'And you've had forty-eight hours at least without your daily fix... Well, if that is what it takes, never let it be said that I shrank from the challenge. Go back to your room and I'll use the internal line because I promise you anything he can do I can do better...'

Leah sucked in air in a whoosh, infuriatingly shattered by the smooth suggestion. 'You pervert!'

Nik groaned. 'It goes against the grain, but I'm actually beginning to pity your blond Adonis. He had—what? Two and a half months? What *did* you do with him? Hold hands, sigh and share deeply meaningful conversations?'

Red as a beetroot now and seething, Leah's teeth gritted. 'None of your business!'

'But you see me here . . .' Nik spread expressive brown hands in a movement that blatantly betrayed his savage amusement '. . . enslaved by my need to know every gory detail.'

Quivering with rage, Leah turned on her heel. 'I'm hungry,' she said in a frigid voice.

'Not for him, you weren't. Maybe you were hungry for a little attention and romance. I can understand that,' Nik drawled in the tone of one attempting to hold a deeply meaningful conversation and struggling.

'You're so bloody basic, you ought to be in a cage!' Leah suddenly slung at him, losing control at the arrogance with which he talked down to her.

'At least I'm trying to understand what attracted you to a third-rate wimp like Woods!' he slammed back at her in a devastatingly sudden explosion of raw anger.

'I've got very bad taste, Nik. Don't you know that? After all, once I chose you.'

Adrenalin was racing through Leah's veins. She saw something in Nik which she had not seen before, and marvelled that she had been so blind. Nik was not jealous of Paul—no, that would have been far too exaggerated a description of what he was feeling right now. But it undoubtedly offended Nik's macho pride to believe that his wife preferred another man to him. Right at that moment it would have killed Leah to admit that Paul was yesterday's news and as third-rate as Nik had claimed.

His brilliant eyes glittered over her and she could feel the raw force of his powerful personality beating down on her. It was oddly exhilarating, not demeaning, as that little scene with the towel had been that day in Paris when Nik had fondly imagined that all he had to do was crook an arrogant finger and she would do what he wanted ... willingly, eagerly, gratefully ... the way all the other women had in Nik Andreakis's roving existence.

'You need——' Nik began.

'Well, I *don't* need half my clothes ripped off me like the last time,' Leah cut in, lifting her chin high and shooting him a look of sublime scorn.

The silence lay there, thick and impenetrable, disturbed only by the thump of her own heartbeat in her ears.

For a split-second Nik stared at her with black eyes as dense as the night and then his sensual mouth gave a sudden appreciative twist and he threw back his dark head and burst out laughing. Sharply disconcerted, Leah stared back at him, colour flooding her cheeks. Without warning, she felt achingly vulnerable.

As she made a hurried movement to walk away, he caught her back with a powerful hand and guided her into the room he had recently vacated. 'You said you were hungry. I'll order some food,' he said, abruptly prosaic.

But not a prosaic man, she reflected as she was thrust down unceremoniously on a comfortable sofa across from the cluttered desk he had clearly been working at. She linked her not quite steady hands, ruefully conscious of the internal upheaval that resulted from being in Nik's radius. You never knew what was likely to happen next. Once that had fascinated her. He was so different from her. They were night and day, chalk and cheese. And yet when he had laughed she had been made shatteringly aware of the electrifying charisma that was so innate a part of him.

Why should she be surprised by that? Why should she feel threatened by that acknowledgement? Nik was devastatingly good-looking ... sexy, very sexy. He couldn't help being like that. She had watched him at dinner parties, the effortless cynosure of all female attention.

He took it for granted. It had always been that way for
Nik, she imagined. His mother and sisters probably
worshipped the ground he walked on too. So really it
was only natural that she should also be aware of that
natural magnetism, should find momentarily that the
ground lurched almost dizzily beneath her on receipt of
one dazzling smile... Yes, it was only natural wasn't it?
It didn't mean anything, just that she was female and
alive.

'I'm glad that you are feeling stronger but you look
very serious,' Nik drawled.

Leah took a deep breath. As she glanced up, she caught
the dancing remnants of humour in his clear gaze and
her mouth ran dry. Nik in charm mode—well, that was
a new one to her, wasn't it? Deliberately she fixed her
gaze to one side of him. 'We need to talk.'

Nik laughed softly. 'The hour is too late, *pethi mou*.'

Her husband, the chauvinist pig. Any minute now he'd
be telling her not to worry her pretty little head about
anything. Nik, she appreciated with a stab of pain, had
never taken her seriously. Maybe he never took any
woman seriously or maybe it was because she was small
and blonde and once she had been crazy about him and
he knew it.

But five years ago Nik had put her on ice. He had left
her to exist in limbo, neither free nor married. And in
that interim it had not occurred to him that her feelings
might have changed. He had not been interested in her
feelings. He had been far too bound up in seething resentment and bitterness even to spare a thought for what
she might be suffering.

It had not occurred to him that she might turn to
another man. It had not occurred to him that she might
be willing to sacrifice the financially privileged lifestyle
that being an Andreakis gave her to gain her freedom.
Nik had falsely assumed that the money and the status

were very important to her. And those were the barriers she had to breach.

'Nik, we have to talk, and, if it's possible, without you getting angry, threatening or sarcastic,' Leah murmured tightly.

Nik was lounging back against the edge of his desk, surveying her with an air of maddening indulgence, the same way that one might look at a child struggling to be amusingly mature beyond its years. And yet she could sense tension within him on another level.

'Nik——'

'Your meal.' At spectacular speed, Nik strode across the room and whipped a tray from a dumbstruck manservant.

Leah was equally astonished. Had it been anyone else but Nik, who had all the sensitivity of a battering-ram, she would have thought he was being deliberately evasive.

'Eat.' The tray was placed on her lap.

'Nik, I know about you and Eleni Kiriakos.'

He swung back to her, a frown-line pleating his winged ebony brows. 'Ponia,' he guessed grimly. 'What do you know?'

'I understand that you were engaged to her.'

'For years,' Nik conceded with disorientating casualness.

Leah looked at her exquisitely arranged salad with sinking appetite and lifted the cutlery. 'Well, I can understand how you must have felt when Max put you in a position where you had to break that engagement and lose the woman you loved.'

'The timing was inconvenient . . .'

Leah lifted her head. 'Inconvenient?' she echoed half an octave higher.

Nik released his breath with impatience. 'I have known Eleni all my life. We were betrothed in our teens. The decision had nothing to do with us. It was what our fathers wanted, a merger between two shipping lines.

Eleni wanted to be a doctor. Her father did not approve but my support brought him round. Both Eleni and I knew that eventually we would have to disappoint our families but in the interim it suited both of us to play along——'

'Play along?' Leah questioned.

'If I had said that I did not wish to marry Eleni her father would have pressured her to marry someone else and she might never have got to study medicine,' Nik explained, his mouth twisting. 'You must understand that Eleni is a dedicated doctor who gives virtually one hundred per cent to her vocation. She has time for little else. She is not the wife I would have chosen for myself, nor was I the husband she would have chosen...'

Leah swallowed hard, striving to absorb his calm assurance and tie it in with what she had believed she had seen in that hospital. Close friends embracing? Eleni had been so affectionate towards Nik but then people who had known each other all their lives tended to be and possibly it had been some time since they had last met, Leah reasoned uncertainly under the onslaught of Nik's level scrutiny. His cool candour was impressive, she had to admit.

'You weren't in love with her?'

'I believed I was once.' Nik smiled with wry recall. 'But I was only eighteen. Eleni was beautiful. That was all that mattered. But it was not very long before her absorption in her studies made me see that we were incompatible.'

'You wanted her one hundred per cent vocation to be targeted on you.'

'You know me so well.'

'Frankly, it was just an observation,' Leah said stiffly. 'Why did you call the timing of our marriage inconvenient?'

'Eleni's father blamed my defection on her dedication to her career and she was forced into open conflict with her family before she had won her independence.'

'And how did your family react?' Leah heard herself prompt tautly.

'With shock, horror and shame at my behaviour,' Nik enumerated flatly. 'A betrothal is a serious commitment in Greek society, most particularly to a family as steeped in traditional beliefs as mine. I was accused of dishonouring the Andreakis name. It is true that inevitably the betrothal would have been broken but the fact that I immediately married someone else magnified the offence in their eyes.'

Leah studied the carpet and she saw her father like a cold force at the centre of a storm, wielding the elements within his grasp without caring about the damage he inflicted. 'I'm sorry,' she sighed.

'It's immaterial now. Last year Eleni married another doctor.' Nik's strong features tautened. 'Both families were placated by that development. If they do not concede that we had a right to choose our own partners, I do believe they both acknowledge that Eleni and I would not have been suited.'

Leah began picking at her salad, a little embarrassed at her dramatic assumption that Eleni Kiriakos was Nik's mistress. A newly married woman, a lifelong friend. Why should she not have openly demonstrated her fondness for Nik? Perhaps she had misinterpreted what she saw because she had never been in a position to offer anyone that kind of affection. Her father hadn't wanted it. Nik hadn't wanted it. By the time Paul came along, she had been inhibited by the habit of concealing her emotions.

The silence lingered. Deep in thought, Leah ate her meal.

'You close me out as if I'm invisible,' Nik murmured silkily. 'When you do that I want to smash things and shout.'

Her silvery head flew up, stark confusion etched in her sapphire eyes. 'That's childish.'

Nik shrugged a broad shoulder with magnificent unconcern. 'There is a child inside every one of us.'

Leah cleared her throat awkwardly, strangely disconcerted by that unexpected admission and the ease with which he'd made it. Living with Nik, she decided, was like camping out on the side of a live volcano. There was always a rumble, a warning quake of suggested disaster in the air.

'Why won't you let me go?' she demanded starkly.

'You're my wife.'

'Not good enough.'

Nik spread beautifully shaped fingers. 'That certificate is still out there,' he reminded her drily.

Leah paled. 'But my father is dead ... he probably destroyed it!'

'He destroyed nothing else,' Nik pointed out. 'And Max was very clever. I may have despised him but even I have to acknowledge that. Who knows what he might have arranged? If we split up, if we part, somebody somewhere may be primed to use that certificate to hurt my family——'

'That's being paranoid!' Leah muttered unevenly, her head beginning to ache.

'It's not a risk I am prepared to take. As far as Max was concerned you were content to be my wife right up until the day he died,' Nik said smoothly. 'He knew no different. And I believe that he would have taken a special pleasure from ensuring that if I ever attempted to divorce you I would pay.'

The most obvious explanation had evaded her, she conceded dazedly, her hands clenching tightly together. She had let her imagination run riot. She had believed that Nik might well be punishing her for her father's sins. She had believed that Paul's very existence so outraged Nik's pride that he was set on hanging on to her out of sheer dog-in-the-manger bloody-mindedness. She had even begun to believe that on the basis of practical, unemotional reasoning he might indeed consider her to be a suitable wife.

And the terrible reality was that every one of those motivations had been considerably kinder to her ego than the awful truth she had finally been forced to acknowledge: Nik thought he was stuck with her for eternity. Like an albatross. And if he hadn't been so accustomed to being in that position he might well have been wondering whether a suitably choreographed accident might not best meet his requirements.

'You've turned a little...pale,' he mused.

'I've got a headache,' Leah mumbled.

She was remembering the fury which had brought him to her hotel, a fury which she now saw had been entirely divorced from any personal feelings on his side. After all, Nik *couldn't* allow her to leave him. Even if he really wanted to throw the door wide and encourage her to leave, he couldn't risk doing it. Marrying her had indeed been the life sentence he had called it.

For the first time she understood how furiously helpless he must have felt in the grip of that awareness early on in their marriage...and how desperately he must have hoped that *she* would meet and fall for someone else while her father was still alive, thereby releasing him from the union. After all, had that been *her* choice, Max could scarcely have blamed Nik. No wonder he had left her alone for five years...and no wonder he had accused her in Paris of being obscenely faithful and loyal. Why had she chosen not to examine that condemnation more closely? Why had she buried it?

The tray was removed. Nik bent down and began to lift her. 'I can manage!' she gasped strickenly, but he ignored her.

Settled back on the bed, Leah snatched at the sheet and turned over on her stomach, unable even to look at him. She felt stripped of every ounce of pride, every inch of dignity. She was drowning in humiliation. In the space of minutes Nik had changed everything. What right did she have to demand her freedom now? Whether she liked it or not, it had been her infatuation with Nik which had trapped him into this situation. Even Max wouldn't have tried to push her into marriage with a man she neither wanted nor loved.

'You'd feel more comfortable without that robe.'

Leah tensed, having been unaware that he was still in the room.

'It doesn't matter.'

'You need a good night's sleep.'

She felt the sheet move, hands at her waist, gently tugging loose the sash and then sliding the robe down off her shoulders to remove it. The sheet was smoothed back into place.

Nik sighed softly. 'You know this is *my* bedroom. Would you mind very much if I moved back in?'

Leah went rigid and then quivered. 'I'll move now,' she managed, beginning to lift her head.

'I want you to stay,' he breathed in a curiously stifled tone.

'Oh...' Leah froze, violently disturbed by the announcement.

'We are married,' he murmured.

The silence stretched, gnawing at her every nerve-ending.

'Yes.' It was a whisper so faint that the sound of a pin dropping would have been louder. But it was an acknowledgement which Leah had avoided, protested and denied for years. Now it had been forced on her.

She lay there in shock. There was no other word to describe her condition. The sturdy foundations of her resentment and bitterness and her determination to leave him had been blown to smithereens and right now she was still lying in the bomb crater, fumbling feebly to find some reasonable excuse for denying him the right to sleep in his own bed and the expectation that she share that same bed. And the truth was that there wasn't any reasonable excuse available to her.

Nik had come to terms with their future that day in Paris. She saw that now. He had got to the bottom of that safety-deposit box and emerged without the ticket to freedom he had vainly sought. For a little while he had hoped that *she* had it—that wretched certificate that she had never even heard of before that day! And when he had realised that unpleasant reality he had known simultaneously that their marriage was indeed a life sentence. Hence his sudden change of attitude towards her. If escape was out of the question, he had to make the best of imprisonment. If he could not free himself to marry another woman, he had to make the best of the one he had got...

All of a sudden Leah was shorn of defences. Hadn't she brought all of this on them both? Hadn't she, in her complete and utter stupidity, agreed to marry a man who had looked like death warmed up on the day he had proposed? And she had asked him if he was ill. *Ill*? Three weeks had passed before the wedding and she had only seen him twice in company and he had been so cool and so distant, he had been like a stranger. But had she smelt a rat? No way! She had been head over heels in love and had told herself he was preoccupied with business.

A slight sound dredged her from her frantic lashings of self-loathing. She turned her head. Her lowered lashes swept up, revealing startled blue eyes. Nik was undressing. Tension thrumming through every tautened muscle, Leah closed her eyes again. But she listened, just as she listened minutes later to the sound of the shower running. Ordinary, everyday sounds for most married women...only not for her. And she found herself envisaging the state of the bathroom: a heap of discarded wet towels and nothing used returned to its proper place.

She had a stark memory of having once invaded Nik's wing of the London house after he had departed one morning. She remembered the wet towels, the disorder and the disturbing, frightening realisation that no two people could have been more separate or less intimate than they were in their marriage that was not a marriage.

After that she had felt like a lodger in his beautiful house. She had never stamped her personality anywhere, never moved a single piece of furniture. That day had been the beginning of her detachment from him... just as this day had forever shattered that same protective device.

Her ears pricked up in disbelief at the sound of Nik humming a brief snatch from a famous operatic aria out of tune. He sounded so... buoyant? Her lashes lifted. She clashed unexpectedly with gleaming jet. Nik was standing by the bed gazing down at her. Instantly his gaze veiled, the curve of his expressive mouth straightening out.

'Go to sleep,' he instructed almost soothingly.

She closed her eyes, heard him discard the towel which was all that had interrupted her view of that lean, lithe golden body. The mattress gave ever so slightly, the sheet slid and then the light went out.

Silence fell. Leah lay as still as a corpse but considerably more wide awake, knowing that she could not possibly sleep with Nik lying naked within a foot of her, his every restive movement filling her with instinctive alarm and rocketing tension.

Wonderfully warm and relaxed, Leah gave a sinuous little wriggle and the hard heat of the body next to hers tautened. Her lashes lifted. She looked up into smouldering black eyes, fringed by ebony lashes. The impact of those eyes was mesmerising. Her blood leapt in her veins and her heat raced. She felt dizzy, breathless and utterly dispossessed of all rational thought.

A fingertip stroked along the lush ripeness of her lower lip. 'Open your mouth for me. I want to taste you,' Nik urged huskily.

Held fast by his searing gaze, she instinctively obeyed and with a stifled groan of satisfaction he crushed her slender form to him, his hands sweeping over her hips and her back as his hard, demanding mouth took hers with savage intensity.

A sweet, twisting ache stirred in her belly. The tip of his tongue snaked between her readily parted lips, erotically probing the tender inner reaches to make her quiver with helpless excitement beneath him.

With insistent hands Nik tugged the thin straps of her nightdress down from her shoulders, baring the pouting swell of her breasts. His sure fingers cupped and explored the straining mounds and caressed her nipples until they were throbbing and stiff. Uncontrollably her hips arched up to his, her thighs trembling in response as her hands rose and tangled in his thick black hair.

Her heart hammered wildly in her chest as he released her reddened lips. He teased her sensitised breasts, his tongue skimming down the valley between them while his hands toyed with the rigid peaks he had created. Heat was surging through her in waves of violent response and when he employed his mouth on her tender flesh instead she moaned low in her throat, subjected to a storm of exquisite sensation that tantalised and tormented.

She was intoxicated, enslaved by passion, lost in a world of intense and drugging pleasure. With a soft growl of anticipation, Nik took her mouth again with compulsive hunger and pulled her against him, his hand sliding through the silvery curls at the apex of her thighs, searching out the silken softness beneath with intimate expertise, each sensual invasion calculated to heighten the fevered and mindless response he was receiving.

It was a sweet agony of delight that made Leah sob and pant for breath. Her hips jerked and lifted of their own volition, the demanding ache of desire rising to an unbearable pitch. A whimper of frustration was torn from her. His hands sank beneath her as he slid between her thighs. He threw back his head and raised her to meet the powerful thrust of his hard body. With an earthy groan of unashamed pleasure, he drove his rigid, swollen length into her yielding depths.

Leah felt her body stretch to accommodate his raw invasion, the sensation still new enough to shock, and then he moved inside her, creating an insatiable need that burned through her entire body. Unconsciously her fingers dug into his smooth, muscular back, her breath sobbing in her throat with every urgent thrust. Ecstatic sensation took over as he possessed her so thoroughly that she was driven out of her mind with sheer, splintering pleasure. And when release came it consumed her utterly for long, timeless moments and then dropped her down gently into sweet, drowning languor.

'Heaven is said to come to he who waits,' Nik murmured silkily, curving her confidently into the damp, hot heat of him. 'But I was always a speculator... and patience is not one of my virtues.'

Exhausted, satiated, Leah couldn't think straight, and while her mind was endeavouring to function again she slid back into sleep. When she wakened again the curtains were wide, the sun high in the sky and a breakfast tray, its contents congealing now, lay on the cabinet on her side of the bed. She looked for Nik, found him gone, and felt dismayingly alone.

It was midday but as she dived out of bed all that she could think about was the events around dawn. Her crumpled nightdress lay in a heap on the carpet like an accusing statement and a flush of shame flamed over her skin, a sigh of intense mortification dragged from her as she looked at the evidence in horror.

He had woken her up, he had deliberately woken her up out of a sound sleep and ensured that she didn't have a chance to consider what she was doing! She washed herself from head to toe in the shower but she couldn't wash away the intimate ache that reminded her of his lovemaking.

Why did she blame him? she asked herself abruptly. Why did she keep on kidding herself that he was the only one responsible for what happened every time he touched her? The truth was that when Nik touched her she melted, she burned, she craved with a wanton lack of control that was so obvious to her, it could scarcely be a revelation to him. Without the smallest effort, he had taught her to want him before she'd even known what wanting was.

Five years ago that instinctive desire had made her uneasy, embarrassed and stilted in his presence. She hadn't been ready for that intensity and when Nik had left her to sleep alone it had been a relief to close out those disturbing sensations which had once afflicted her whenever he was close. But when he had chosen to smash down that wall she had put up in self-defence he had unleashed a flood of passion as powerful as a tidal wave.

For she had never stopped wanting him any more than she had denied herself the ludicrous responsibility of buying his socks. The one personal thing she had ever done for him and she had clung to it right to the bitter end. God, it was so pitiful; little wonder he had laughed. Nik probably had more socks than Imelda Marcos had had shoes. Tears stood out in her anguished eyes as she saw inside herself.

Some rejected women clung, she had bought socks with the compulsion of a fetishist, fixed stupid flower arrangements in his wing of the house to remind him of her existence, turned herself slowly but surely from an

unsophisticated teenager into one of the most elegant
women in London. There wasn't a bit of her she hadn't
made over for his benefit. It was pathetic to love a man
so blindly—utterly, unforgivably pathetic.

For she did love him. She had fought that love with
Paul and denied its existence, unconsciously fighting for
the freedom that her pride demanded. And nothing had
changed. Nik didn't love her, never would love her. He
was just stuck with her. On his side the sex was
merely... merely functional. He woke up in bed with a
female body and what happened next was one of the
very few things that was entirely predictable about Nik.
So she needn't start telling herself that her husband had
suddenly begun to find her an unbearable temptation.
Nik was a very virile male and he wasn't given to soul-
searching over something as basic as his sexual needs.

But he wouldn't let her go unless that certificate turned
up and for the very first time Leah was consumed by a
need to know more. Was it a marriage certificate, a birth
certificate, a share certificate...? Dully she enumerated
several more possibilities. The first two were unlikely,
she decided. Nik had said he was protecting his family.
He had never mentioned himself, so had someone com-
mitted some sort of crime in his family? Embezzlement,
financial skulduggery?

Sheathed in a cunningly cut blue dress, she walked
out on to the wide terrace that overlooked the sea and
the cliffs far below. In any other mood, she would have
wanted to take in the spectacular view and explore the
rest of the house but her sole driving compulsion was
to find Nik. He was standing on the terrace, dark and
lean and lithe in tailored cream chinos and an open-
necked black shirt. As he heard her steps, his dark head
turned.

She hesitated under the full onslaught of his night-
dark eyes, indeed was so wildly disorientated that she
very nearly cannoned into a lounger near by. Colour

flooded her cheeks, an aching, terrifying awareness quivering through her slender form. She couldn't take her eyes off his starkly handsome golden features and was plunged into instant recall of how she had felt in his arms hours earlier.

He dealt her a dazzling smile and strode fluidly towards her. 'How do you feel?'

'Fine...'

'Just fine... You look spectacular,' he murmured with a slightly ragged edge to his deep, dark voice. His eyes ran over her in a blatantly possessive scrutiny, taking in the fall of silvery hair, the delicate perfection of her glowing face, and roamed right on down to her toes, taking unashamed note of every curve he found *en route*. 'Glorious,' he added, reaching for both her hands and drawing her close.

Her heart pounded and she tried to steady it, bewilderment in her sapphire eyes. 'Nik——'

'And mine,' he completed with intense satisfaction.

Everything she had intended to say went straight back out of her head again.

'Am I interrupting something?' Ponia asked chirpily, causing both their heads to spin round.

'Not at all.' Nik smiled, releasing Leah's hands just as she attempted to snatch them away.

'The staff are hovering with lunch,' Ponia explained, watching Nik swing out a chair by the table and settle Leah into it.

Leah was conscious that her hands were shaking. The full effect of Nik's warmth and admiration had shaken her. But it couldn't mean anything. Maybe he was always charm personified with a new lover. For that was really all she was. New, fresh, different in every way from the women he usually took to his bed. And the charm wouldn't last. Women bored Nik easily, quickly. She had always known that.

Lunch was served. Ponia chattered about inconsequential things. Every time Leah looked up from her plate she was entrapped by Nik's slumbrous gaze and her pulse would quicken and her temperature would rise, making her reach for her wine with increasing regularity.

Nik's mobile phone buzzed. He left the table to pick it up where it lay on a chair several yards away.

'I can't wait until the rest of the family see this,' Ponia chuckled.

'Sorry, I . . . ?' Leah dragged her attention from Nik's vibrant smile in her direction as he talked into the phone. It was no mean feat.

'You're locked into each other like a pair of magnets on a honeymoon. When I invited myself along I had no idea what I was getting into!' Ponia grinned to show that she wasn't offended. 'I'm going swimming. I'll see you later.'

Hot-cheeked, Leah bent her head. She grabbed up her wine again. It gave her something to do with her hands. She had come out here to talk seriously to Nik, a challenge at the best of times but a positively mountainous challenge when, for the very first time in five years, he was treating her like a highly desirable woman and being shatteringly attentive.

Draining her glass, she stood. Nik curved his arms round her from behind, taking her by surprise. As he tugged her relentlessly back into contact with the abrasively masculine angles of his powerful form her treacherous body quivered with an instantaneous response which terrified her and she tensed.

'What's wrong?' he breathed from above her head.

'There's something we need to discuss——'

'Forget it. If the discussion is likely to harbour a single mention of divorce, separation, celibacy or Woods, let me give you a hint,' he said with sudden harshness. 'Keep your mouth closed.'

An entirely unexpected spurt of amusement assailed her. He always thought he was one step ahead of her and for once he wasn't. 'It's not about any of those things.'

Nik tugged her round. 'Then it's not important.'

Before she had even guessed his intention he was covering her mouth hungrily with his own. It was headier than the wine she tasted on his lips, sweeter than anything she had ever known. Helplessly she leant into him, snaking her arms round his neck to stay upright, the flames of her response burning up every skin cell. His fingers splayed beneath the curve of her hips, lifting her into electrifying contact with the unmistakable thrust of his erection.

'I want you again,' he muttered thickly.

And she wanted him so badly there was an ache low in the pit of her stomach, her mind suddenly a shameful receptacle for erotic images that were shatteringly new to her experience. But the very strength of the passion he could evoke within her devastated her. He didn't even have to use pretty words or compliments. He didn't even have to make an effort. A few kisses and she simply fired into spontaneous combustion. Like a sex toy, a submissive little doll that he could manipulate wholly to the dictates of his own needs. That image gave her the strength to pull back from him.

'I have to talk to you,' she framed, and turned towards the house. 'And I think we should go inside.'

'We can talk in bed.' Nik tracked her with predatory black eyes.

'You only got out of bed a few hours ago!' Leah heard herself hiss.

'And I can't wait to get back there, *agape mou*.'

How did you switch him off again? she wondered wildly, dismally conscious of the tautness of her nipples and the tingling heat deep in the very heart of her. It occurred to her that if she was programmed for his benefit he was very much programmed on the same wave-length and that if she relaxed her guard for one tiny second he was intent on taking advantage of that.

'I think you're over-sexed,' she whispered, sharply disconcerted by what was happening between them.

'And you're complaining?' He dealt her a smoulder-ing smile.

Leah attained the cool of what appeared to be the main reception-room, perspiration beading her short upper lip. She sank down on a sofa.

'*Theos*, that's so cute! Your feet don't touch the floor!' Nik laughed and, instead of picking another seat as she had hoped, crouched down in front of her. 'So talk,' he invited, studying her with heavy-lidded eyes.

Feeling cornered, Leah edged further back into the depths of the sofa. 'I've been thinking——'

'Dangerous...definitely a habit you have to break,' Nik interrupted mockingly.

She had to steel herself to continue. 'About that certificate.'

He uttered a very rude word she had never heard pass his lips before. Hard tension locked his strong features into immobility and he sprang upright and strode across to the stone fireplace. 'You do pick your moments,' he said grimly. 'What can we possibly have to talk about on that subject?'

'It has to be found...and I thought that maybe if you gave me some idea about what that certificate contains——'

'No!' He shot her a forbidding look and she suffered a weak moment of piercing regret for the speed with which his mood had altered.

'I wouldn't tell anybody, for goodness' sake!'

Nik regarded her with pure steel in his hard gaze. 'The fewer people who know, the safer my family is.'

She noticed something that a mere day earlier would have left her untouched. She noticed that she did not figure as a part of his precious family. 'You don't trust me.'

'Trust doesn't come into it.'

'And the last person you're likely to trust is Max Harrington's daughter,' she completed painfully.

'I didn't say that——'

'You didn't need to. You treated me like a leper for long enough!' she added helplessly.

'The past is behind us——'

'How can you say that when you're expecting me to live with it?' she demanded unevenly, her sapphire gaze bright with pain. 'I thought that maybe if I knew more I might be able to help you find that certificate...'

'Ah...suddenly I understand.' He slung her a glittering look of slashing derision, his hard jawline clenching fiercely. 'You see it as your passport to freedom. Come up with the certificate and I set you free? Is that it?'

Her narrow shoulders rigid with strain, Leah forced herself to meet that savage scrutiny but she could feel the blood draining from her tense face. 'Isn't that what you want too?'

'I wanted it so badly I could taste it five years ago!' he delivered with cruel candour. 'And a week ago I thought I had that certificate. But something changed for me when I emerged empty-handed from that filthy box. I knew I had reached the end of the road and I refuse to waste another single day brooding over a fruitless search. It's over now!'

'No, it isn't,' she dared unsteadily, tears springing to her distressed eyes but willed back with every ounce of her self-discipline. 'Not while we are still together.'

'You weren't thinking of that when I was inside you,' he breathed with raw contempt. 'Or when you were sobbing with satisfaction in my arms.'

'Please,' she gasped, defenceless against the charge, shaken by his explicit reminder of her complete lack of restraint.

Closing the distance between them in two long, punishing strides, Nik clamped his hands over her shoulders and dragged her upright. 'In my bed you're as hot as hell for what I can give you. You love everything I do to you, you love everything I make you feel. With me you're wanton, abandoned and out of control...'

Leah shivered violently, stunned by the attack she had somehow drawn down upon herself. 'How can you speak to me like this?'

'You can be a whore in my bedroom any time and I don't give a damn about how you conduct yourself in the kitchen or the drawing-room!' he misquoted with seething emphasis, his lean fingers biting into her narrow bones, dark eyes flailing her shattered face. 'But get rid of your adolescent fantasies of true love in a cottage with Woods. It's never going to happen unless I'm six feet under! You're my wife. Face it and face it fast before I lose all patience with you!'

The door slammed thunderously in his wake. Leah dared to breathe again but her heart was pounding against her ribcage in near panic. Nik had exploded into rage like a bonfire rained on by paraffin. Dimly it occurred to her that she might have been wiser to tell him that Paul no longer featured in what he had called her 'adolescent fantasies'. But that idea was wholly crushed as she relived the humiliation of the verbal attack she had just been forced to withstand.

'Hot as hell...wanton...abandoned...a whore'. No doubt it was exactly what she deserved. She had reduced herself to his primitive level, allowed herself to forget every principle and every decent inhibition, number one of which should have been no sex without love. Well, he could just go back to his bimbos, then; it was absolutely no skin off her... Yes, it was, it was! Deeply hurt, positively savaged by the very idea of Nik with another woman, Leah vented a stifled sob and fled.

CHAPTER SEVEN

'Is NIK working?' Ponia enquired gently over dinner for two.

'Probably.' Leah contrived a stiff little smile meant to suggest that she had only just noticed his absence and was quite unconcerned by it. After all, she reminded herself doggedly, five years of almost continuous absence ought to have accustomed her to the value of her own company and counsel. Only somehow it hadn't. Their relationship had changed so fast and so radically that Leah was in turmoil and her desperate attempts to regain her former detachment weren't working one little bit.

'He was in the taverna this afternoon; one of the fishermen at the harbour mentioned it,' Ponia supplied, and looked uncomfortably at Leah. 'He's in a rage, isn't he?'

'We had an argument, yes,' Leah conceded, wishing that the teenager would drop the subject.

'He has a very hot temper.' Ponia pushed her thick curls back from one small ear, a reflective curve to her mouth. 'But he very rarely loses it—which is just as well, considering that the family just don't know how to handle it. My grandmother never raises her voice. None of them do. They go white to the gills and back off when Nik blows up. The one and only time I saw it, it fascinated me.'

Nik's niece was watching her almost expectantly. Leah's brow furrowed but she said nothing.

Ponia concentrated on her plate but kept on talking. 'I was about eleven when I overheard my two aunts talking about Nik. They were wondering who his natural parents were and I didn't even know what that meant then——'

Leah froze. 'His natural parents?' she repeated, carefully keeping her voice level.

The teenager's face was uncharacteristically serious. 'Of course, I was stupid enough to go and ask my mother and she was really upset. It was years before I understood that adoption's only something to be ashamed of in *my* family.'

'Yes,' Leah agreed, since some input appeared to be expected from her. She was so afraid of revealing her astonishment that she wouldn't even let herself think about what she had just learnt.

Ponia visibly relaxed. 'It's never, ever mentioned. Everybody outside the family thinks Nik was born to my grandmother; how did she get away with it? She was forty-eight!'

'It's not impossible.' Leah was becoming uncomfortable although she could understand Ponia's curiosity. Her request for an explanation of what she had overheard at eleven had obviously been greeted with maternal dismay and distress and a brick wall of silence. She was a lively, intelligent girl, still clearly troubled by the response she had received.

Ponia shrugged. 'The secrecy must have made it much harder for Nik.'

'People are much more open about adoption now than they were thirty years ago.' Leah took a deep breath. 'But we shouldn't be talking about this, Ponia. It's too private and, before you ask me, no, I don't know anything more than you do.'

Ponia went a fierce red and bent her head. 'I'm sorry. I don't know why I brought it up——'

'Because I'm family... and yet not family,' Leah supplied gently. 'But I think you have to accept that Nik has a right to privacy about something that personal and

I may be wrong but I doubt that it would be a good idea to raise the subject with him.'

'I wouldn't dream of it.' Ponia was aghast at the idea.

Leah smoothly changed the subject and hoped she had firmly dissuaded the younger girl from further indiscreet probing. But long after Ponia had said goodnight Leah was bothered by what she had been told. In some ways she knew nothing about Nik and that hurt; no matter how unreasonable that was, it hurt. She wandered into the drawing-room where she had noticed the magnificent grand piano earlier in the day and sat down on the stool.

So Nik was an adopted Andreakis. And it was foolish to feel hurt that he had never even made a fleeting mention of the fact. After all, it was blatantly obvious that his family had gone to some lengths to conceal the adoption. His parents had had three daughters and must have badly wanted a son. And in a veil of secrecy they had adopted a baby boy. Over the years Leah had read several profiles on Nik in the newspapers and not one of them had referred to that. Ponia was right. Nobody outside the family circle knew.

What age had Nik been before he learnt the truth? Had his parents been more honest in private than they had been in public? If they hadn't been, it must have been one hell of a shock, she reflected, her fingers moving nimbly over the gleaming keyboard, the rich virtuosity of a Chopin concerto flooding the room with the music she often employed to accompany her deepest thoughts.

She hoped Ponia had the sense to be discreet. Some secrets you just had to live with. Maybe Nik didn't want anybody to know either. Or maybe he simply didn't give a damn, considered it scarcely relevant to his adult life. He was very attached to the family she had yet to meet. He was capable of very strong emotions. Why had she never seen that before? A male capable of marrying a woman he didn't love merely to protect his family was a male capable of putting other people's needs ahead of his own. Although it was a little hard to appreciate his sacrifice when she had been part of the burnt offering.

Dear God, she thought, with a surge of sudden pain, how could she exist in a marriage where nothing was given or shared but a bed? It was too late for her to accept that. Maybe years ago, when she hadn't known any better, hadn't known Nik for the man that he was, she would have happily settled for what he was prepared to give her. But not now, when every sense craved more.

But she had no choice, and even if she did have a choice, did she really have the strength to walk away from him? Was half a loaf better than no bread? She lifted her hands from the keyboard in sudden bitter distress.

'Don't stop...'

Her spine rigid, Leah slowly swivelled round on the stool. Nik was standing in the shadows by the window. A shimmering tension emanated from the tautness of his stance; his black eyes glittered in his dark face. His hair was tousled, his shirt half unbuttoned, his jawline blue-shadowed.

'Play for me,' he said roughly, and it was not a request.

Leah spun back round to the piano. Her sapphire eyes flared. She lifted her slim hands and played 'Chopsticks', every deliberately discordant note expressing her mood of defiance.

A set of hard fingers closed round her narrow wrists and jerked them up. Sudden silence spread through the room, broken only by her own fractured breathing. She could feel the warmth of his powerful body, raw with tension, mere inches from her as he bent over her. A shiver ran through her.

'Why?' he grated, releasing her wrists.

'I'm not your slave,' she muttered shakily, but that wasn't why. She remembered playing for him years ago, remembered that first night; she had never played for him since. Music had always been her mode of self-expression. It had become far too personal to share with Nik.

'*Play*,' he said again.

Her hands were trembling. The atmosphere was dangerously charged with every forceful element of Nik's volatile temperament.

'I have no music.'

'You can play for hours without music,' he reminded her harshly.

Enervated by his louring presence, she began to play, snatches of this, pieces of that, but her usually nimble fingers were reluctant to do her bidding smoothly and several jarring notes disturbed the performance. After the fourth mistake her fingers slid from the keyboard.

'You're very stubborn. I should have realised that,' Nik breathed. 'You may look as fragile as spun glass but you're not.'

But right now Leah felt very fragile. Every nerve-ending was singing with the high-wire tension in the room. Slowly she stood up, reluctant to look anywhere near him.

'So tell me about him,' he invited dangerously quietly.

Her head spun round, silver hair flying back from her delicate cheekbones. He had cut off her intended exit route. 'I don't know what——'

'Your lover...' Eyes dark as an abyss rested on her expectantly.

A frisson of alarm snaked through her. 'You can't possibly want to hear about Paul.'

'Can't I?' Nik challenged, treating her to a lethal smile that was pure unalloyed threat. 'Where did you meet him?'

'Harrods.'

'*Harrods*?'

'He knocked me over and insisted on buying me a coffee,' she stated curtly.

'You let yourself be picked up in Harrods?' Nik murmured incredulously.

'He did not pick me up!'

'In Harrods,' Nik said again as if he couldn't believe it. 'And where did it go from there?'

'It didn't go anywhere from there,' Leah returned with spirit. 'I ran into him again the next week——'

'Let me guess...same day, same time, same place——'

'I don't remember.'

'You were hoping to meet him again.'

Leah said nothing. She walked across to the window and stared out at the blackness studded by stars above the shimmering sea. Nik had no right to ask her such questions; no right, she told herself fiercely.

'So this electrifying affair began in Harrods,' Nik drawled. 'Where in Harrods?'

Something snapped inside Leah. 'What the heck does it matter *where*?'

He lowered himself down on to a sofa and stretched out his long, lean legs in an attitude of goading relaxation. 'I'm trying to get a picture. Was it in Ladies' Lingerie or the food hall?'

'I refuse to dignify that with an answer.'

'Much better to leave it to my imagination,' Nik agreed silkily. 'So tell me how he worked his way on to my territory.'

Leah's teeth clenched. 'Very easily.'

'Temper, temper,' Nik purred. 'I wasn't there. That's the only reason he found it easy.'

And she knew then that she would not admit that her relationship with Paul was over, her much vaunted love nothing more than an infatuation. Nik's arrogance inflamed her to the brink of spitting and clawing like an enraged cat. Paul was her one defence and she needed that defence. God forbid that Nik should guess that something more than sexual need had fired her in his arms. Life would absolutely not be worth living if he realised that she was in love with him.

She recalled his slashing contempt in the car that day in Paris when he had believed that she still loved him and inwardly she shrank from the threat of ever giving him that weapon.

Loving Nik didn't make her blind. He was ruthless. He would use anything and anybody for his own ends. And this inconceivable love which should have died a decent death years ago was a weakness which made her vulnerable.

Maybe she was one of those crazy, sad women who associated love with pain, a victim of her own conditioning. How else could she explain how she felt about him? Right now she was so furiously angry with Nik that she wanted to scream and yet she was equally aware that on some twisted level deep down inside her she was enjoying the fact that he was with her, his entire attention focused on her to the exclusion of all else. And that acknowledgement just made her feel ashamed.

'You don't love him,' Nik murmured softly. 'If you had loved him you would have slept with him the first chance you got.'

Infuriated by his persistence, Leah spun back to him. 'Believe it or not, some of us are capable of practising self-restraint!'

Nik shifted like a lunging tiger cat on the sofa and angled deceptively slumbrous eyes over her angry face. 'You don't practise it around *me*.'

The awareness that she had walked right into that smooth reminder outraged her.

'Not that I'm complaining.' Nik sent her a glittering smile that burned over her sensitive skin like acid. 'Rampant lust appeals far more to my natural instincts than eyes meeting across a crowded basket of Brussels sprouts. It was the Food Hall, wasn't it? True romance blossomed among the veg. *Cristo*, I am riveted by the sheer cliff-edge excitement of such an encounter.'

'Paul has more romance in his little finger than you have in your entire body!' Leah slung at him in shuddering rage.

'Yes, he bought you coffee ... I'd have taken you to the nearest hotel and poured champagne over your beautiful breasts and I can assure you that you would have found that far more exciting.'

Leah went white, stabbed by savage pain from an unexpected source. She had no problem envisaging Nik in such a role. Suddenly she wondered how many women had had champagne poured over their breasts by *her* husband. Her stomach churned. She dealt him a look of icy distaste. 'Don't get me mixed up with your bimbos. I'm going to bed!'

And not *his* bed either, she decided hotly, snatching up a few necessities on her stalking progress through the master bedroom suite and out again.

Fifteen minutes later she was ensconced in a bed at the far end of the corridor behind a securely locked door. They might be stuck with each other but she didn't need to sleep with him! In fact, she would have had a whole lot more respect for herself had she *never* slept with him. What was she ... some kind of masochist? As she had stood there tonight listening to him ridicule her relationship with Paul, she had found out all over again that hate and love were but two sides of the same coin.

A slight noise made her tense and turn over. She was just in time to see a tall, dark shadow drop fluidly and almost silently over the sill of the lowered window. On the edge of a scream, Leah stared in disbelief as a shaft of moonlight illuminated Nik's starkly handsome features.

'Tell me,' he said conversationally, 'is this game of musical beds aimed at adding a little romance to our relationship? Was I supposed to climb in with a rose between my teeth and a box of chocolates?'

Leah unglued her tongue from the roof of her dry mouth. 'There's a two-hundred-foot drop down to the beach out there!'

A flash of white teeth revealed his amusement. 'And wouldn't you have had a lot of explaining to do if I'd fallen?'

Her lashes fluttered. He was quite untouched by the horror which had enclosed her the instant she had registered the risk he had taken. An unthinkable, illogical risk for anyone as prudent as Leah. But not for Nik. Nik thrived on danger. Nik loved to be challenged. 'You are c-crazy!' she gasped, feeling quite sick as she thought of what could have happened.

'Kicking in the door wasn't an option with Ponia under the same roof. And it would have brought the servants running. I would hate to embarrass you like that.'

'And kicking in a door wouldn't embarrass *you*?' Leah countered, so taken aback by his behaviour that she couldn't think straight.

'Not if it was the door to my wife's bedroom and it was locked,' Nik fielded, calmly shedding his clothes in an untidy heap. 'For a Greek, that is grounds for extreme provocation.'

'You might have bloody well killed yourself!' Leah suddenly heard herself scream at him, on the brink of physical attack. 'And would it have been worth it?'

'Nik slid into the other side of the bed and angled a feral smile at her, all teeth and macho self-satisfaction. 'Ask me in the morning,' he suggested, reaching for her.

'*No!*' Leah shrieked, backing off so fast that she fell out of the bed with a bone-jarring thud. 'If you're sleeping here, I'm sleeping somewhere else!'

'You don't sleep with me, you sleep on the floor.'

'Like hell I will!' she blazed back at him. 'What do you think I am?'

'No bimbo ever gave me this amount of aggro,' Nik sighed, lazing back against the pillows. 'You're holding out for an apology for what I said this afternoon——'

'I'm *what*?'

'But what you took as an insult I see as a compliment,' he drawled smoothly. 'Find me a married man who doesn't want a passionate wife and I'll show you a liar.'

Leah shuddered. His innate deviousness only further inflamed her. 'You called me a whore.'

'I did not. I said you were welcome to behave like one in my bed... any time,' he completed huskily.

'No, thanks!'

'Although you would need a few lessons to make the grade,' he murmured with naked provocation. 'And I can hardly wait to give them to you. What more can I say in my own defence?'

Leah drew in a shaky breath. On a level she did not want to examine, Nik fascinated her even when she was furious with him. But then no natural born womaniser with his looks had ever won notoriety without an equally natural flair for the field. He had tremendous charisma when he chose to exert it. But she fought the awareness as she fought him.

'We can't live together like this——'

Nik sprang back out of bed. 'But we've only just begun. Come here...' He reached for her and caught her up in his strong arms before she could retreat.

'No——' The raw force of his mouth silenced her, the strength of his hunger catching her unawares. Her hands balled into fists and struck out at him and then the hunger caught her too. It was like being swept up by a tidal wave. His tongue prised her lips apart and probed within, sending waves of instant excitement flooding through her taut body. The blood raced in her veins, heat exploding like a sunburst deep in the very heart of her.

The percale sheet was cool on her back as he laid her down on it. A convulsive shiver racked her. She looked up at him, a kind of desperation in her beautiful eyes even as he smoothed a possessive hand over the pouting swell of her breasts and her heart lurched violently against her ribcage, the sensation tearing a response from her which she couldn't hide.

'This isn't what I want...' she whispered fiercely, fighting the drowning desire which threatened her.

'But you want me.' Smouldering dark eyes struck hers on an almost physical collision course, denying her concealment, holding her gaze entrapped.

'No!'

'Yes.' The hard, vibrant contours of his face were uncompromising. He played with her lips and she tasted the tang of whisky on his breath as she accepted the sudden thrust of his tongue, sudden pliancy, sweet as honey, flooding her susceptible body as he held her on the heights of anticipation with the skill of an expert lover. 'You want me...you want *this* as much as I do...'

A stifled moan was wrung from her as he dropped his dark head and covered a taut nipple with his mouth, making every muscle she possessed jerk tight in instant, terrifying reaction.

'Admit it,' Nik demanded, sinking his hands below her hips and pulling her to him.

'Yes...*yes!*' It was a cry of defeat as she surrendered to the hot enticement of his mouth and his sure hands but deep down inside her she feared that she had just given up something vitally important to her own survival...

CHAPTER EIGHT

LEAH sat on the beach with her arms wrapped around her raised knees, watching the surf whisper up on to the shore. The eternal rhythm of the waves was soothing. Heat beat down on her, filling her with languor. In a matter of days her skin had turned a pale gold under the kiss of the sun. How many days... ten, eleven? She didn't know. She had stopped watching clocks and studying calendars. Nik was *here*, not about to arrive, not about to depart, not about to leave her alone for endless weeks, and that knowledge filled her with an increasing sense of security.

She was happy, and sometimes, as now, when she was briefly free of the spell cast by Nik's vibrant proximity, being so happy frightened her. Looking back down through her life, she could never recall feeling like this. And if she allowed herself to think of the ruthless practicality which had motivated Nik into making their marriage a real marriage she marvelled at her own contentment.

But then she loved Nik Andreakis. If she kept her pride and her fear of the future out of the balance, it was natural that she should be happy when he spent practically every hour of the day with her, when he made love to her over and over again with an insatiable hunger which made her feel like the most desirable woman in the world. So, she had compromised her own ideals; so what? she asked herself.

Nothing was perfect; nothing was without flaw. When you got down to basics, she had what she had always wanted. She had Nik. She was his wife. She probably had more of him than any other woman had ever had. And he was behaving like a husband. He was starting to talk in terms of 'we...us...ours', no longer separate in thought and deed but patently rearranging his thinking to see them as a couple. And that was a big stride for him.

Close family or not, Nik was very much a loner, and she had never seen that in him until now. The extrovert front concealed that inner wariness of his. He found it so much easier to be sarcastic than candid where emotions were concerned. Deep down inside he had an innate reserve which astonished her. It was so foreign to the arrogant, brash image of him which she had cherished for years.

Why didn't she just admit it? she asked herself. She smiled and let her fingers trail through the silky sand. She was more in love with Nik than she had ever been. He had told her that they could have a very good marriage and this far he had proved his point. Did it really matter that he didn't love her? He *wanted* her...all the time. Her cheeks burned. But would that last? Would it be enough for him? Would he get bored? A year from now, where would they be? That was an answer nobody got to know in advance, she scolded herself.

Crunching footfalls interrupted her troubled thoughts and she turned her head. Dimitri, one of the youngest of the household staff, was crossing the beach towards her, laden with what looked like the provisions for a picnic lunch. He greeted her in careful English and then with great ceremony proceeded to spread an immaculate cloth over the sand. Two bottles of wine in cooling-sleeves and crystal glasses were produced.

'Kyrios Andreakis will be here directly,' Dimitri imparted, and hovered with the corkscrew.

'Thank you. I'll see to the rest. It looks gorgeous.' Leah peered into the yet to be unpacked box and her mouth watered. 'Cook has surpassed herself.'

'I not wait, *kyrie*?'

'There's no need.' With difficulty, Leah hid her amusement as he laid down the corkscrew with a deep air of uncertainty. Just for once Nik could open the wine and they could serve themselves.

It was their last day on the island, she reflected sadly. Tomorrow they were flying to Athens and she would meet the rest of his family. Ponia had returned home a few days earlier. Leah had protested until the girl had grinned and said, 'Two's company, three's a pair of lovers and one gooseberry!'

Nik strolled across the sand towards her, blatantly aware of her intent absorption in his approach, and he smiled, unashamedly basking in her appreciation. In a pair of faded, tight cut-off jeans and nothing else, he looked nothing short of spectacular but there was something about that smile, something about that light in his lustrous dark eyes which clutched at her heart and squeezed it hard.

For an instant, an almost boyish vulnerability was etched in the electric charge of his answering appraisal and then it was gone, wiped out by a thick cloaking veil of ebony lashes that any woman would have killed to possess, and she told herself she had imagined it.

'You're wearing white,' he murmured, dropping down beside her in a sprawl of long, golden limbs. 'It suits you.'

'I was wearing white the first time you saw me.' She didn't know why she said it; it was just one of those instant thought connections which flew off the tongue.

Nik tensed and lifted the corkscrew. 'Yes.'

It was not something he wished to discuss. He didn't have to tell her that. Nik could put out warning flares without opening his mouth. Impulsively, she ignored the atmospheric vibrations. 'You went to a lot of trouble to meet me——'

'Did I? Give me your glass.'

Leah nibbled at her lower lip and lifted both glasses, her attention resting on the set line of his sensual mouth as he poured the wine. Frustration coursed through her. He shut her out, held her at a distance. The closer they got, paradoxically the more he withheld, as though he didn't trust her. And why should he trust her? She was an idiot. How did she expect Nik to trust her when he no doubt believed that in some corner of her heart she was still pining for Paul?

Why hadn't she told him the truth yet? Pride? Ego? Or the fear that Paul's very existence had partly spurred Nik into claiming her as his real wife? Nik was highly competitive, possessive, territorial. Keeping her pinned like a specimen butterfly to a board for five years hadn't bothered Nik but when the butterfly flapped its wings and without warning tried to fly away he had been challenged, not to mention staggered by the idea. Take the challenge away, tell him he had vanquished the opposition . . . would he lose interest? That was what had kept her quiet and suddenly she wasn't very proud of that reality. Game-playing wasn't very wise with someone as volatile as Nik.

'This is for you.' A fancy little box was laid beside her bare toes.

Leah gave him an astonished glance and lifted it almost shyly. She flipped open the lid and the sunlight glanced blindingly off the sapphire and diamond ring within. Slowly she breathed in and drew it out. 'It's exquisite,' she whispered a little hoarsely, turning to look at him again.

Faint colour emphasised his hard cheekbones. 'It's an eternity ring.'

'Yes.' She swallowed the thickness of tears in her throat. 'I know.'

'Why are you shocked? It's just a present. Drink your wine before it gets warm,' Nik urged with a rough edge to his voice.

He knew damned well why she was shocked. Apart from the wedding-ring proffered at the altar, Nik had never given her anything but money. Christmas and birthdays, great fat inputs into her bank account, nothing to unwrap, nothing to get excited about, an acknowledgement of her existence and his wealth, nothing more. She had bought her own jewellery and when a piece was admired at a dinner party she would say, 'Nik bought it for me,' reasoning that that was not a lie when it was his money which she had used. But now the memory of that proud and empty pretence just made her want to cry.

'You don't want it,' he condemned with an abruptness that startled her and made her flinch.

'Of course I do!' Without any hesitation, she threaded the ring on to her wedding finger for she had the terrible suspicion that if she didn't move fast he would snatch it off her again and throw it out to sea.

He released his breath in a hiss, the harsh angle of his jawline easing, and she realised that he was, if anything, even more on edge than she was and guiltily aware of those five years of impersonal cash influxes.

'Dad used to give me money too,' Leah shared flatly. 'It's OK. I never expected anything else. The only time he ever gave me a present——'

'Me?' Nik vented a grim laugh, his expressive mouth twisting. 'And I wasn't much of a gift, was I?'

'I was going to say, the only thing he ever gave me was my mother's writing bureau.' Her smooth forehead furrowed. 'And you know it's not at all valuable. It's pretty but he wasn't remotely attached to it. In fact it was kept in one of the attic rooms and he had to have it restored but he said... Nik, do you know what he said?' she muttered with growing excitement.

'I'm not remotely interested!' he asserted with sudden impatience, clear frustration mingling with other intense emotions in his lean, hard features as he reached for her, determined to gain her full attention. 'I'm trying to tell you that...' Uncharacteristically, he hesitated. '*Theos*, I wish I hadn't spent five years being a self-centred, arrogant bastard, making you pay for what Max did...although I didn't see it like that at the time!'

His lean fingers were biting into her narrow wrist, eloquently betraying just how hard he found it to admit such sentiments. And the writing bureau which Max had told her to 'guard well' simply evaporated from her mind.

'But I can understand why you behaved that way...*now*,' Leah murmured wryly.

Nik grimaced. 'You were only seventeen and you were infatuated with me.'

She dropped her eyes, her skin heating, and drank her wine.

'And I think even then I accepted that you were innocent of all knowledge of your father's blackmail. I could have been kinder. You were little more than a child. You were far more naïve than Ponia is at the same age. When I saw you together here...I saw things I didn't want to see five years ago,' he completed in a constrained undertone.

'It doesn't matter now,' she muttered, troubled by his introspective mood.

'I must have hurt you a great deal.'

'Yes.' There was little point in denying it. 'But I got over it.' Forcing a smile to her not quite steady mouth, Leah sat up on her knees and reached into the box of food to begin unloading it. 'What would you like——?'

'You...now!' Nik breathed rawly without warning.

Reaching up, he pulled her down again with two impatient hands. He laced long brown fingers painfully tightly into her silky hair as he gazed down at her startled face with incandescent black eyes. 'Forget the food,' he added with a sudden ragged intonation she recognised, only this time it combined apology with desire.

And she did forget, the same instant that he brought his mouth swooping down into explosive connection with hers. The smooth control she was accustomed to was absent. Nik unleashed a passion that devastated her. It was no slow, gentle seduction of the senses but an erotic assault in which clothes were thrust aside rather than removed. Excitement took over, blanking out everything but her body's insanely instinctive need for him.

She gasped and threw her head back as he drove into her, rejoiced in his answering groan of satisfaction and from that point on there was nothing but wild sensation, rising to ecstatic heights she had never touched before and finally throwing her over the edge into a shattering release.

Nik mumbled something in Greek, his arms closing convulsively round her as she stirred. 'Did I hurt you?' he breathed unsteadily.

He had shocked her, she acknowledged, unable to resist sending a possessive hand travelling over his damp brown back, feeling his muscles flex in response. But then Nik frequently shocked her, both in and out of bed. She was getting used to it. A rather dazed smile curved her lips as she uttered a reassuring negative.

'*Theos mou* . . . I could lie like this all day.' Sliding on to his side, he carried her with him and viewed her with slumbrous dark eyes and an undeniable air of indolent satisfaction. 'Every time I look at you you get more beautiful, *agape mou*. At seventeen you looked like an angel, pure, untouchable. Now you look like a woman, your mouth swollen from my kisses, your hair in a mess,' he murmured, his sensual lips curving with rueful amusement, 'and you still take my breath away.'

'Do I?'

'How can you doubt it? The last time I made love on a beach I was a teenager.' He pulled her up with him and cast her a mocking smile. '*Now* we eat.'

All his tension had gone. He had said what he obviously felt he had to say. He had expressed regret for those five years. Guilt had taken a long while to hit him, but then, it was only now that Nik actually *felt* married, only now that he could make the effort to understand that he had not been her father's only victim.

Max had been too shrewd a man not to foresee Nik's resentment and bitterness at being forced into marriage and he could hardly have failed to be aware that Nik had other women. But Max hadn't cared, hadn't asked questions, hadn't worried that she might be unhappy, Leah acknowledged painfully. He had caught her a very wealthy, influential husband and he had been very proud of that feat.

'Why so serious?' Nik probed.

'I was thinking about Max.'

'Wherever he is, he's probably laughing like a hyena right now, you can be sure of that,' he returned witheringly. 'Here we are, doing exactly what he always wanted us to do, and sooner or later we'll even have a child——'

'A child?' Leah was arrested by the concept, eyes wide.

His gaze narrowed, suddenly cool as winter. 'One of those wriggly little pink things which scream a lot and require exhaustive house training,' he extended very drily. 'Most people find their helplessness cute and appealing . . . but maybe you don't.'

She flushed, looked down into her glass. 'I do . . . I just never thought about it,' she muttered unevenly, forbearing to admit that she hadn't thought along such lines in many years. But sudden warmth flooded her as she imagined carrying his baby.

He curved an arm round her, hauling her into the shelter of his sun-warmed body. 'I thought maybe next year,' he imported huskily, treating her to a dazzling smile in reward for having given the desired response.

'It would be rather awkward for you if I refused, wouldn't it?' she said, abruptly rebelling against that arrogant stamp of approval. 'Considering that you're stuck with me anyway!'

'Is that what you think?'

Leah wished she had kept her mouth shut. She could see the ambience of the last few glorious days going up in smoke in front of her eyes. 'It's the truth, isn't it?' she whispered tightly.

'Our marriage is what *we* make of it.' Shifting, Nik enclosed her in his strong arms, turned her round and settled her between his spread thighs. Insistent dark eyes levelled on hers, holding her fast. 'Understand that, accept it,' he instructed. 'Don't look back.'

And then he kissed her and refilled her glass and offered her some food but she wasn't really hungry any more. She watched him eat with unblemished appetite and for the first time she allowed herself to think with optimism about their future. If he could put the past behind him so could she, and maybe the first thing she ought to do was tell him the truth about Paul...

'Nik...?'

At the same time as she spoke someone called down from the top of the steep path that wound down from the villa. Nik uttered an imprecation and sprang upright in a movement indicative of his raw impatience. 'I said *no* calls, *no* interruptions!'

She watched him stride closer and shout back. Then he spread his hands in a gesture of exasperation. 'Urgent,' he grated. 'It had better be very urgent! Stay here... wait for me.'

He went up the path at speed. Leah helped herself to some luscious strawberries which had caught her eye. She studied her ring from all angles and smiled, quite euphorically happy all of a sudden. It was an effort to recall that she had to tell him about Paul when he returned because in all truth, she registered sleepily, she just didn't want to remember how foolish she had been.

She woke up to noise, startled, disorientated. She saw a helicopter far above, hanging like a giant black bird, a second before it swept out across the bay. Pushing her hair off her hot face, she frowned down at her watch. She had been asleep for a couple of hours and Nik hadn't come back.

Dimly she remembered the phone call—at least she assumed it had been a phone call. An urgent one. Clearly urgent enough to make Nik forget about her. She discovered her panties and pulled them on with a rueful giggle, tugging down her dress again, feeling deliciously abandoned.

She strolled into the cool of the villa and noticed the silence. She laid down the picnic stuff she had hauled up from the beach. The staff seemed to have vanished. An odd little shiver ran up her backbone—a premonition that something was wrong. Nik was in his office, studying something on his desk.

'You forgot about me but I forgive you,' she teased uncertainly from the doorway.

He raised his dark head and straightened. Eyes as treacherously cold and threatening as black ice focused on her and right there and then, in one devastating second, Leah knew that sixth sense had not betrayed her. She could feel the suppressed rage he was struggling to control, see it in the rigidity of his golden features as he stood there staring her down with all the silent intimidation he was capable of transmitting.

Leah paled. 'Is there something wrong?'

'How *did* you guess?' His deep voice shook perceptibly with the force of the emotions he was visibly tamping down.

'What is it?' Her heartbeat had shifted up into the region of her throat.

'Come here,' he murmured flatly. 'I have something to show you.'

She had a terrible craven urge to run away but she quelled it and crossed the room.

Then she saw them—would have had to be blind to miss them. A collection of glossy photographs was fanned out across the desktop. Leah blinked, leant closer, steadying herself with one small hand. Her stomach gave a violent lurch and dropped down to somewhere near her toes. Shock reverberated through her. The photos were of her and Paul.

In disbelief she stared and pushed one aside to examine another... and then another. Paul and her walking hand in hand down a crowded street, kissing in the wine bar, glued together in a doorway, smiling euphorically at each other. She squirmed, feeling as if Jaws had jumped out of a puddle at her and bitten a large chunk out of both her lower limbs. Her knees threatened to fold. Her eyes stung painfully. *Why now*? she wanted to scream in a sudden surge of anguished resentment. Why now when they had been so happy?'

'Where did they come from?' she whispered sickly.

'Did you know that you had a photographer on your trail?'

'No...'

'Do you know what photographs of my wife with another man are worth on the open market?'

Her marriage? Leah looked numbly into space, temporarily shorn of reaction by shock. In spite of all her ridiculous precautions she had been recognised, followed and captured on film. And not once had she even suspected it.

Nik quoted a fantastic sum and then waited as though he expected some kind of response. She made none; could think of absolutely nothing to say.

'These photos were offered to one of the tabloids,' Nik grated. 'If the owner of that rag had not been one

of my closest friends and his editor aware of that fact
they would have been published!'

'You bought them,' she gathered, a slender hand lifting
to press against her throbbing temples.

'You're my wife! What choice did I have?' he raked
at her with raw aggression, every bitten-out syllable expressing his fury. '*Cristo*!'

'Stop shouting at me!' she gasped in growing distress.
'I'm sorry about this but I couldn't have stopped it happening...and anyway it's *over* with Paul! It was over
before I walked out on you in London. I probably should
have told you that before now——'

'Spare me your lies,' he cut in with ruthless, icy
precision.

Leah froze, lifting darkened eyes to his. 'I'm not lying.
It *is* over.'

'You would tell me anything to protect him. I see that
here!' A brown hand slammed down on the photos in
emphasis. His glittering gaze was alight with cold hos-
tility, his handsome mouth compressed with distaste.

'You're not listening to me...you don't believe me,'
she whispered dazedly.

'It's unimportant, immaterial,' he dismissed in a tone
that cracked like a whiplash. 'But never in my life have
I been more humiliated!'

Her relationship with Paul was 'unimportant, immaterial'? Her throat closed convulsively as she gaped
at him. Paul meant nothing at all to Nik? She saw her
cosy, silly fantasies about their marriage shatter into
pieces around her stupid feet, exposed by hard reality.
Nik was only concerned about his public image, his
macho sense of honour, his hypocritical belief that, while
it had been all right for him to celebrate his extra-marital
interests abroad, she should have been above reproach.

She felt sick. All at once she deeply regretted her attitude of guilt and apology. Her sole desire had been to
limit the damage caused to their relationship but now

Nik had made it brutally clear just how empty a charade their marriage was on his side.

In a surge of pain, she lashed out. 'If you call *this* humiliation, you've had a very easy ride through life!'

He stilled. The silence of his disbelief pulsed like a live wire between them.

Leah lifted her head and clashed with glittering jet eyes. Something had snapped inside her. 'I've had five years of humiliation in newsprint...everybody knows just how much you valued your marriage, Nik. You made very sure of that. But when the boot is on the other foot it's suddenly a hanging offence. Just be grateful you had the connections and the money to save face; I had neither,' she told him with bitter dignity. 'And I had to stand the pitying glances and the innuendoes of your guests at your dinner parties as well!'

He had gone white, his strong bone-structure prominent beneath his golden skin. 'I did not consider myself married.'

Leah cast a speaking glance down at the wretched photographs, refusing to betray her embarrassment or her anguished regret. 'Well, neither did I——'

'That is different.' Nik did not yield a logical inch, he was still in such a rage.

'Yes, I was more sensitive,' Leah conceded shakily, sudden tears of turmoil threatening and willed back. 'And too much of a coward to do anything about it. But I'm not going to bow my head like a sinner and I'm not going to say sorry either——'

'*Theos mou*...' He slung something at her in guttural Greek, both fists clenched.

'Because I'm not sorry. In fact in the mood I am in now I wish your friend had printed them and you had to live for just a few weeks with what I had to live with for five years!' She threw back at him in a wild surge of bitterness and distress. 'Surprised, Nik?'

'You bitch...' Breathing rapidly, he stared at her with sudden total impassivity, as if he had switched off every emotion. A faint tremor ran through him, a dark rise of blood accentuating the savage slant of his hard cheekbones.

'But then it's just one of those things a *man* couldn't possibly understand. A stage I had to g-go through.' She slung his own cop-out back at him with helpless venom, wanted to shut herself up and discovered that she couldn't. 'And, just like you, I went through it later than most! Only I wasn't as sneaky, slippery and downright devious as you are about justifying yourself and I never set out to deliberately hurt or humiliate anybody! I was too busy being what you call a "lady"...and much good it did me turning the other cheek!'

He swung on his heel without a word and left her standing there alone, shaking and sick inside, wondering dazedly where all that spite had come from. From inside her, she registered in shock. Five years of suppressed bitterness and pain had leapt out when it was least welcome and she knew exactly what had sent her over the edge.

Nik had been solely concerned about the threat of a loss of face. A tremendously important issue to a Greek with both feet still set squarely in the Neanderthal caves. His precious pride, nothing more in the balance. He had wanted her sobbing for forgiveness at his feet. Nothing less would have satisfied. The very last thing he had expected was defiance and a reminder of his own indiscretions. One rule for him, another for her.

Leah covered her hot face with spread hands, a feeling of despairing emptiness enclosing her. Once more she had made an outsize fool of herself. Nik had had to dissuade her from walking out again. So he had swept her off to bed, switched on the charm...and she had fallen for it hook, line and sinker! It had taken a crisis for her to see just how little she really mattered to him. And dear God but it hurt; it hurt so much to be forced to face the reality that the man she loved didn't give a damn about her.

CHAPTER NINE

THE limousine travelled at a snail's pace through the heavy Athens traffic. Out of the corner of her eye Leah noticed Nik helping himself to a drink. He passed her one without being asked. She drank without examining the contents. It tasted like pure orange. Meanwhile the silence smouldered. The atmosphere was explosive. She felt like a straw doll with a flame-thrower aimed at her. Menace threatened on all sides.

Where had he slept last night? When she had finally drifted off around dawn she had still been alone. He hadn't put in an appearance at lunch either, not that she could say that she had been disappointed by his absence. It had taken ice cubes, cold cloths and every cosmetic technique she possessed to conceal the reddened state of her eyes. She didn't feel in any fit state to meet Nik's family. Her nerves were jangling like piano wires.

When she simply didn't think she could bear the silence one minute longer, she settled on what she saw as a safe subject. 'When we get back to London,' she murmured tautly, 'I'm going to check out that writing bureau. It's a long shot, I know, but Max did tell me to guard it well. It might just have a——'

'Secret drawer? Or maybe a hidden coded map with X marks the spot?' he cut in in a growling tone dripping with sarcasm. 'I doubt if Max was as deeply into Enid Blyton as your imagination appears to be. Take an axe to it if you like! It won't get you anywhere.'

If it killed her she would find that certificate, she swore to herself, her cheeks burning. It wasn't fair that she should be held hostage to protect someone in his precious

136

family from having some past transgression exposed.
And it was positively paranoid of Nik to fear that even
though Max was dead that secret might still be a threat,
likely to be dragged out into the light of day if they broke
up!

Parting her lips tremulously, Leah expressed that latter
belief out loud. Nik slung her a seething glance, ne-
gating her assumption that she had chosen a safe subject.
'That is not a risk I am prepared to take.'

'I'm starting to think that you're covering up a murder,
something really ghastly!' Leah shot back shakily.

'Nothing so dramatic.' He vented a harsh laugh, his
jawline clenching hard. 'Your conscience may rest in
peace.'

'I wish you'd tell me,' she said unsteadily.

'And put temptation in your way? Do you think I don't
know how desperate you are to be free? Do you really
think I'm that stupid?'

Leah paled but she defended herself. 'I wouldn't hurt
your family.'

'Wait until you meet them,' he breathed with dark
satire. 'You are not about to step into a living, breathing
episode of *The Waltons*.'

Leah tensed. 'And what's that supposed to mean?'

'You'll see.'

He lounged back into the corner in one fluid motion,
black eyes shielded to a sliver of light in his impassive
face by the thick dark crescents of his lashes. His expressive mouth had a decidedly embittered curve. It
finally dawned on her that he was not looking forward
to an ecstatic family reunion. Or was it that?

Why did she continue to ignore the fact that those
wretched photographs had been as much of a shock to
him as they had been to her yesterday? New and fragile
bonds had been shattered by too brutal a reminder of
the recent past.

And in her determination to defend herself she had used those photos as an excuse to vent her own bitterness. Maybe she had chosen the wrong issue on which to make a stand... and very possibly the wrong target as well. It wasn't Nik's fault that she was still furiously angry with herself for not trying to take control of her own life sooner, for playing the martyr to the bitter end to retain her father's approval, and, finally, for being taken in by someone as superficial as Paul Woods.

No, Leah had to face that that frustration, regret and humiliation had all been self-induced. Nik had played little part in her passive acceptance of a marriage which was a charade. He had taken his lead from *her*. That was a devastating truth for her to accept but she saw that it *was* the truth, and what made it worse was the fact that she had long been happy to avoid it.

Not once in five years had she objected, demanded or even attempted to discuss the situation and Nik had not been in a position to demand his own freedom. Little wonder that he had decided that she was either obsessed with him or determined not to lose the status and wealth which being his wife had granted her.

So only now did she try to imagine how *she* would have felt presented with Nik in a series of intimate photos with another woman... She would have felt *savaged*. But Nik had never done that to her. He had been discreet. He had never featured in a clinch with another woman in newsprint. There had been no kiss-and-tell revelations—plenty of gossip-column inches of suggestion but never any actual proof that he was intimately involved with any of his beautiful companions.

Besides, whether she liked it or not, Nik had had a right to say that he had not considered himself married then. Forced into marriage with a seventeen-year-old, he had simply got on with his life as best he could. He had never been unkind to her. He had never set out to hurt her. In front of other people he had accorded her every respect. He had given her the status which her father had demanded as the price of silence. What more could she have expected? Love hadn't been part of the deal even then. And one way or another she would have to learn to live with that.

'Yesterday——' she began, without even knowing what she intended to say but painfully aware that she had to make an attempt to bridge the gulf which had opened up between them.

'I wanted to kill you,' Nik murmured flatly.

Her head jerked. His sculpted profile was as emotionally uninformative as his intonation.

'But then I didn't realise how bitter you were. I don't think I ever looked at those years from your point of view before. You always appeared content...ludicrously content,' he acknowledged, with a wry twist of his eloquent mouth. 'But you never betrayed any sign of unhappiness.'

Leah laced her unsteady hands together. 'You weren't there to see it and I learnt how to hide my feelings.'

'Why did you stay with me? I *have* to know that,' he breathed, turning hooded dark eyes on to her without warning. 'I'm well aware that it couldn't have been my wealth, not when you were prepared to give it all up to be with Woods. So why did you stay for so long?'

Faint pink burnished her cheeks and then drained away again under the onslaught of that probing scrutiny. She veiled her eyes and opted for honesty. 'The first time I saw you...' She uttered a jerky laugh. 'It sounds so stupid now but for me, well, it was love at first sight.'

'That doesn't sound stupid,' he said.

God, this was so embarrassing and he was trying to help her out by acting as if what she had just said was not embarrassing. But talking about feelings did embarrass Leah. It had been so easy to say 'I love you' to Paul when he had said it first. Nothing further had been required from her.

'Has it ever happened to you? I mean, like, at first sight?' she muttered almost inaudibly.

'Yes.' Nik then provided a slight hiatus by choosing to lift the phone and communicate with his chauffeur in Greek before continuing. 'It was instantaneous and as terrifying as jumping out of a plane without a parachute. I felt out of control, taken over. I didn't like it.'

Disconcerted by his candour, Leah bent her head, knowing that he was talking about Eleni Kiriakos. He had only been eighteen, she remembered that. But still it hurt to know that another woman had been capable of rousing that kind of emotional intensity in Nik. And no doubt had Eleni been less preoccupied with her medical studies Nik would have stayed in love.

'You were telling me how you felt,' he reminded her.

Leah bit her lip and tasted blood. 'I was so naïve... At the beginning I thought you felt the same way. You were only flirting but I didn't have the experience to recognise that,' she said brittlely. 'So you can blame me entirely for what Max did. If I hadn't fallen for you and made it so obvious, he would never have thought of dragging any skeletons out of closets.'

'That wasn't your fault. I know that I blamed you that day at the bank but I was lashing out at the easiest target,' he admitted with unusual quietness. 'You were not to blame but you were Max's daughter and the pressure I had been under since his death combined with the discovery that that box did not contain what I sought made me lose my head. It may be coming a little late but I am sorry for the manner in which you learnt of your father's ... trade.'

'I had to find out some time.' Confused by his soothing manner and simultaneously surprised that they *still* had not arrived at his mother's home, which she had vaguely understood to be no great distance across the city, Leah stole a glance at him, and was further bewildered by the intensity of his appraisal.

And then comprehension hit her. Naturally Nik did not wish to introduce her to his family when they were obviously at daggers drawn, so he had evidently buried his own anger in an effort to paper over the cracks for the sake of appearances.

'I think it's very important that we should be honest with each other,' he asserted, lowering his dense black lashes. 'You say that you loved me when you married me...when did you stop?'

'Stop what?' Inexcusably her attention had strayed as she'd looked at him. He could stop her heart dead in its tracks just with one smile. And he was right—it was terrifying to love like that, to lurch from the heights of heaven to the depths of hell, to have one's entire hope of happiness centred solely on one person... and in this case a volatile and ruthless individualist as difficult to read as a blank canvas.

'Loving me?' Nik pressed with impressive casualness, almost as if they were discussing something as impersonal as the weather.

Leah tensed. Somehow—and she didn't quite understand how—she had stumbled into a nightmare conversation. 'I just shut you out...I don't remember when——'

'So why did you stay?'

His persistence was remorseless. Yet she could understand his need to know. Her lashes screened her eyes. 'Marrying you was the one thing I ever did that made my father proud of me...that was one reason. I was very hooked on trying to win his love and approval,' she muttered with audible self-loathing. 'Just as at the start I was trying to win yours...'

He released his breath in a sharp hiss.

Leah was in a what-the-hell mood now. Why pretend, why struggle to conceal the obvious? She loosed a jagged laugh. 'Look, it really doesn't matter now. I wasn't trying to make you feel bad but, you see, it was your bad luck

that I was the way I was then. Max always ignored me
and then you ignored me. It was no big deal. It was what
I was used to—my whole life set out for me, a nice safe
little cocoon——'

'But I hurt you... I must have hurt you continually.'

Nik sounded so strange, his normally deep, rich voice
hoarse, as if she was upsetting him... A ridiculous idea,
she reflected, sipping at her drink and wondering why
her head felt so light. He might have regrets for the way
he had treated her in the past but there was absolutely
no reason, in the peculiar circumstances of their marriage, for him to be upset.

'If you don't have high expectations or enough self-
respect,' she muttered tightly, 'you accept being kicked
in the teeth because somehow you think you've asked
for it. And I *certainly* did.'

'You did not ask for one tenth of what I put you
through!' Nik swore fiercely.

Leah stopped staring into space and stared at him instead. He was driving a set of lean brown fingers through
his thick black hair, his strong jawline set like granite,
his normally glowing complexion pale. 'Why should you
feel guilty?' she demanded in open confusion. 'We
weren't really married.'

'But we are married now...' Breathing rapidly, Nik
subjected her to a disturbingly intense scrutiny. 'Your
glass is empty. Let me get you another drink.'

Her head was swimming slightly, she noticed. She felt
oddly detached. If it hadn't been ridiculous, she would
have suspected that she had had a rather large shot of
alcohol but she was only drinking pure orange. Nik knew
that she had no head for drink.

'Have we driven down this road before?' she enquired, abstractedly noticing a church that looked
vaguely familiar.

'Maybe Giorgios is trying to find a short cut,' Nik
suggested.

'I feel like we've been in this car forever.'

'Deeply meaningful conversations can have that effect.'

'I thought they were beneath you.

'Not when my marriage is at stake.'

Her lashes fluttered. Playing for time, she took another slug of her orange juice before looking up. She just couldn't believe he had said that. It wasn't the sort of thing Nik would say. Lustrous dark eyes were nailed to her, a faint flush accentuating the taut angle of his high cheekbones.

'You know... you're gorgeous,' she murmured like someone talking to herself, the words dragging slightly. And it was true—he was, she reflected, scanning his lean, lithe length and striking dark features, a familiar heat surging up inside her.

Nik slid along the leather seat and reached for one of her hands. 'I want you to forgive me for my unreasonable behaviour yesterday.'

On that strange level where she could sometimes read Nik like an open book she sensed sneaky, slippery, devious insincerity. For some reason he was telling her what he believed she must want to hear but he did not think that his behaviour had been unreasonable. And then the proverbial penny dropped like a brick and she grasped what lay behind his extraordinary conduct. 'My marriage is at stake'.

How on earth could she have forgotten? As long as that hateful certificate was out there, Nik was determined to stay married. Yesterday, for the first time, she had stood up to him, *really* stood up to him, and seemingly he was now afraid that she might choose to walk out regardless of the possible consequences to him and his family.

A tight coil of pain snaked up inside her. 'You don't have to say that... I over-reacted. I was embarrassed, maybe a little insensitive...'

'A *little*?' Highlights of gold flashed through his expressive eyes and for a split-second he both sounded and looked much more like himself until he screened his gaze and tightened his hold on her slender fingers to grate, 'No, I was the one who was insensitive.'

Mentally she imagined her ears shooting out on stalks to catch such an un-Nik-like sentiment. 'But I——'

'It was my fault,' he interrupted with more than a hint of aggression.

'But I should have——'

'I don't wish to hear another word,' he spelt out, with an incredibly forced-looking smile.

But she could feel the anger he could barely suppress thickening the atmosphere. If only it weren't such an effort to concentrate, she thought, and she was suffering from a peculiar and unbelievably inappropriate urge to giggle like a drain.

'Nik... I'm not going to walk out again.' She felt horribly guilty that he should be forced to such lengths to try and placate her when it wasn't necessary. 'I know I can't... unless I find that certificate——'

'Impossible,' he broke in with a suppressed violence that she quite understood.

'But you'd let me go like a shot if it turned up——'

'That is not quite how I would put it.' His low-pitched response was uneven.

'Uncork the champagne and dance?'

'Now you are talking nonsense,' he groaned, fan-shaped lashes almost hitting his cheekbones as they swept down.

He rescued her glass before she dropped it, set it aside.

'Is that that church again...?' she enquired without great concern, an unfamiliar feeling of insouciance enclosing her. 'Do you think Giorgios is lost?'

Nik swept up the phone and said something to the chauffeur.

Leah flexed her stiff shoulders and kicked off her shoes and then wondered why she had done something so uncharacteristic. She just felt so incredibly relaxed and yet kind of...excitable at the same time. It was the weirdest sensation.

Nik watched her and then he reached for her other hand and drew her closer. Her breathing was fractured, her heartbeat a magnified thump against her ribcage; the blood in her veins was racing. She could feel her breasts straining against the light silk barrier of her bra, the sudden painful sensitivity of her nipples.

The silence throbbed and then in one sudden startling movement Nik dropped his hands to her hips and brought her down on top of him. But he uttered a stifled imprecation and flung his dark head back a split-second before his mouth met hers in what had seemed like a determined collision. He looked like a male in the throes of anguished conflict.

Leah studied him with out-of-focus eyes, her hands braced on his shoulders.

'Nik?'

'You don't know what you're doing,' he muttered raggedly.

'I know what I want to be doing,' she giggled and, leaning forward, she ran the tip of her tongue teasingly along the compressed line of his mouth.

His hands clamped over her forearms as though he was about to thrust her back from him and then, with a harsh groan, he crushed her against him instead. He kissed her with so much passion that he bruised her lips. She loved it, excitement leaping through her in a roller-coaster wave.

Then abruptly he broke the connection and leant his brow against hers.

'I am a sneaky, slippery, devious bastard,' he mumbled thickly, his breath fanning her cheek. 'I am everything you ever called me and right now I would give ten years of my life to make love to you. I'm in agony...'

'But?' She sensed the 'but' coming.

'There was vodka in your drink. You're plastered, Leah.'

'Oh.'

'It was a disgusting thing to do but I was desperate to make you talk...make you relax. Also, the car has been driving round in circles. Please forgive me.'

As she shifted he shuddered, every taut line of his big body betraying not only his tension but also the intensity of his arousal. And Leah laughed because all of a sudden it seemed terribly funny. As swiftly as she grasped what the matter with her was she knew she ought to be outraged by such duplicity but the idea of Nik being reduced to such desperate straits appealed to her far more. You have a conscience.'

'And right now it is killing me,' he confided thickly, knotting two unsteady hands slowly into her hair to prevent her from moving. '*Theos*, it is always like this with you! I want you so much, you could make me beg.'

That frank confession told Leah of a power she had not dreamt she possessed. She was knocked sideways by the concept. It had not occurred to her that he might find her *that* desirable. But Nik was telling her that this wild hunger that could surge up between them without warning was mutual. But then he was a very physical male. It might not be the true love which her adolescent fantasies had centred on but she sensed that she had vastly underrated the extent of her own attraction.

Even so, she argued, 'I don't have big boobs.'

'I beg your pardon?'

'Or legs that go up to my armpits.'

'*Cristo*, I think you're perfect.' He brushed his lips sensually back and forth across hers, a husky growl of hunger escaping him. 'So very perfect, I can't believe you're mine.'

'Tell me more...' she invited, tilting her head back out of reach with a teasing smile.

Taking abrupt note of the fact that the limousine had drawn to a halt in a courtyard, he swore instead. 'We have arrived.'

It took a second or two for Leah to dredge herself back to the real world again. Nik slid her back on to the seat and then suddenly cupped her cheekbone in a possessive palm and extracted another long, lingering kiss that did nothing to aid her efforts to pull herself together.

The fresh air made her feel dizzy. Nik curved an arm around her narrow back and steadied her while she smoothed down the short skirt of her raspberry-coloured suit. 'If I trip over the furniture it'll be your fault,' she complained.

He laughed softly and bent his head. 'You're still weak from the effects of the flu,' he told her smoothly. 'You'll definitely have to lie down to rest before dinner...and being a caring, concerned husband——'

'A *what*?'

'I will naturally accompany you,' he completed even more smoothly.

As he guided her up the flight of shallow steps and through the double doors—already opened wide on to an impressive marble foyer—she dimly marvelled at the speed and dexterity with which he had returned their relationship to its former footing. She was relieved, she was suddenly happy again, but she was just a little intimidated by the ease with which he had performed that miracle.

Ponia appeared, looking frantic and far more formally clad than Leah had ever seen her, with her hair swept up, her tiny frame sheathed in an elegant dress. 'You're so late!'

'We got lost,' Nik said carelessly.

'*Lost*?' Ponia parroted.

'But we found each other again,' he murmured in an aside only audible to Leah.

'Yes.' A tremulous smile flashed across her lips, her sapphire eyes suddenly brilliant in her heart-shaped face.

'Eleni's here,' Ponia said baldly from behind them.

Leah felt Nik stiffen and then he laughed. 'What a delightful surprise!'

'And the whole Kiriakos tribe are coming to dinner,' Ponia proffered in a rush.

'How very civilised,' Nik responded, but he no longer sounded quite so amused.

Leah wanted to ask questions but it was too late. A manservant was opening a door and suddenly they were on the threshold of a vast reception-room which, dismayingly, was filled with people, every one of whom fell silent and turned to view their entrance.

Nik's mother, Evanthia Andreakis, was a regal, still attractive woman who could easily have passed as being a decade younger than she was. She greeted Nik, shook Leah's hand, barely looking at her, and then quite calmly turned her attention back to Eleni Kiriakos, who was seated by her side, and continued to converse in her own language.

It was Eleni who stood up, a faint flush on her perfect cheekbones, to enquire politely after Leah's health.

'I'm very well, thank you.'

'You look wonderful, Nik.' Eleni smiled with real warmth and the abrupt transformation from cool reserve to vivacity quite startled Leah.

Mrs Andreakis signalled to Leah with an imperious gesture of one hand. Ponia was standing beside the older woman, her pretty face set and flushed. 'My grandmother would like me to introduce you to everyone,' she said stiffly.

'Doesn't she speak English?' Leah whispered.

'Of course she does . . . she's just being blasted rude!' the teenager hissed shamefacedly. 'I thought you were supposed to be the guest of honour and then Eleni arrived, and she was obviously invited!'

Leah was ruefully amused by Ponia's partisan sympathies. 'Nik and Eleni are old friends.'

'The family don't see it in quite that light. Eleni and her husband have just split up!'

A maid was serving them coffee in tiny, fragile porcelain cups. Leah was aware of being the covert cynosure of many eyes, but equally aware that absolutely nobody was approaching her.

'Leah . . . did you hear what I said?'

'Yes.'

'Well, they're hoping like hell that Nik dumps you and takes up with her again. It's disgusting,' Ponia hissed. 'That's why you're being treated like the invisible woman.'

Leah wanted to giggle. Whether it was true or simply the produce of a feverish teenage imagination she didn't care. Nothing could touch her in the mood she was in. She was still dizzily remembering Nik's trembling intensity in the limousine. Nik was hers, maybe not in the way she had once naïvely dreamt of but there was certainly enough there to build on . . . and next year maybe a family. An abstracted smile tilted her mouth as she pictured a little boy with black hair and liquid dark eyes.

'You're really not all here, are you?' Ponia was frowning at her.

'Don't worry about it. But please introduce me to everybody.'

Within an hour Leah had met most of the members of the Andreakis family, and almost without exception she had been received with a stilted formality and brevity which would have struck horror into the bones of a daughter-in-law expecting more of a welcome. It slowly dawned on her that Ponia had not been joking. She felt like the centre of contagion in a room full of health fanatics.

And then Nik drifted back to her side, rested a hand supportively on her taut spinal cord and their whole reception of her changed with a speed that was almost comic. Everyone talked to Nik, everyone listened to Nik, but from two of his sisters and their respective adult children she sensed the lack of any real warmth behind their effusiveness towards him. He kept the lot of them, Ponia had told her bluntly on the island. Only her parents were independent of either Nik's financial support or his employment.

'Come and meet my mother,' Ponia urged impatiently.

Ariadne was seated alone at the back of the room, a slender, quiet woman who seemed very nervous. Her hands were tightly clasped together, her whole bearing so tense when she glanced up and saw them approaching that Leah found herself smiling in what she hoped was a friendly fashion. She was already disposed to like Ponia's mother.

'This is Leah,' the girl announced.

'Please sit with me. Have some more coffee brought,' Ariadne instructed her daughter tautly. 'Nik is looking very happy, I think,' she said then abruptly. 'You are happy too?'

'Very,' Leah murmured after a disconcerted pause.

'For so long I wish to meet you... now I not know what to say.' Ariadne gave an uneasy laugh. 'You are very beautiful... and clever, Nik tells me. You are a musician and you speak French and German too. I learn English from my daughter,' she imparted in a rush, treating Leah to an anxious smile. 'Perhaps next time you come to Greece you come visit me. I like that very much.'

'I think I would like it too.' Leah watched Nik's sister send a skittering glance around the room and decided that Ariadne was afraid of being seen to depart from the family line of accepting Nik's wife only on sufferance. 'I became very fond of Ponia while she was staying with us.'

'You were very kind to have her. Nik spoils her...' Her voice trailed away as a tall man with greying hair entered the room and then rose again as she said with perceptible relief, 'Here is my husband, Stavros.'

Leah's gaze narrowed. There was something about the older man's wide smile and the deep set of his eyes which seemed vaguely familiar, and it had almost gone before she grasped it. Momentarily he had reminded her of Nik and she might have commented on the fact had Stavros not broken into instant voluble speech with all the confidence that his wife lacked.

What did she think of Greece? What did she think of the family? He pulled a face, untroubled by Ariadne's gasp. 'You want real Greek hospitality, you come and stay with us!' he told her cheerfully, his deep, carrying voice reaching all corners of the room. 'We love to entertain young people. Sadly we married late and were fortunate indeed to be blessed with a child but our life is sometimes a little dull for our daughter. She thinks we have one foot in the grave!'

Nik crossed the room. Greetings were exchanged. Considering that Stavros was treating him to the warmest reception he had yet had from any of his relatives, Leah was a little surprised by her husband's constraint—but then she stopped thinking altogether when she encountered the ebony flare of his expressive gaze whipping over her then lingering with a devastating effect that she could feel right down to her toes.

'You're looking very tired,' he murmured.

She went scarlet but Nik was already drawing her upright, extracting her from his aunt and uncle's company with social dexterity. She found herself carried off and she glanced back apologetically over her shoulder and glimpsed a very hurt look stamped on Ariadne's face and then she remembered that Nik hadn't actually spoken to his sister at all and she said so.

'Of course I did,' he asserted dismissively.

'I don't think so,' she muttered.

At the foot of a gracious winding staircase he silenced her by hauling her into his arms and kissing her breathless. She emerged from the embrace with starry eyes and an inability to think straight. Quite uninhibited by any fear of being seen by his murderously correct relatives, Nik bent and swept her off her startled feet.

'So what do you think of my family?' he enquired smoothly as he took a first step up the stairs.

'You want candour?'

'I wouldn't have asked otherwise,' he said drily.

'They're ghastly.' And then she groaned and shut her eyes, afraid to look up at him. 'Of course they're probably a lot warmer than they seem!'

'Probably colder.'

Her eyes flew wide. 'Oh, Nik...' she whispered in sudden pain on his behalf.

'Don't be wet,' he told her with a sardonic smile. 'I'm a big boy now.'

'Stavros and Ariadne are really, really nice and they seem to be very fond of you,' she burbled helplessly in consolation. 'And Stavros even looks like you...yes, that was what made me think I'd met him before!'

Nik froze on the sweeping marble landing. 'Are you crazy?' he demanded with sudden ferocity. 'I'm not even related to him!'

Leah blinked. Of course he wasn't, she registered belatedly. Stavros was only a relative by marriage, a brother-in-law, and furthermore... and *furthermore*... 'But you're not related to any of them!' she heard herself exclaim, and the minute she said it she knew what she had done and she wanted to bite her tongue out after one glimpse at Nik's shattered face.

Ten seconds later she was being forced to stay upright on her own power after Nik strode into a bedroom, kicked the door shut with violence and practically dropped her from a height.

'Say that again,' he invited rawly.

Leah gave up the fight and backed off to sink wretchedly down on the foot of the bed. Her eyes swam with sudden tears. 'I'm sorry... I forgot I wasn't supposed to know.'

'Obviously...and for how long have you known?' Nik raked down the length of the room at her.

'If I tell you, you have to promise me that you won't be angry with the person who told me you were adopted.' She practically whispered the word since Nik's reaction to her even knowing was so explosive. 'She thought I knew, you see——'

'She?'

Alcohol didn't aid diplomacy or secrecy, Leah registered dismally.

'Nobody in my family would have told you!' Nik continued harshly.

'Ponia did——'

'Ponia?' Nik surveyed her in blatant disbelief.

Reluctantly, Leah recounted the conversation that the teenager had initiated. Nik shook his dark head in visible shock. 'All this time she has known? *Theos mou*, I never dreamt she knew!'

'I told her that it was a private matter and I honestly don't think she'll mention it again. She was terribly cut up about it,' Leah hastened to tell him, swallowing back her opinion that it was surely unnecessary for such desperate secrecy to be observed.

After having met the Andreakis clan, she could well imagine them behaving as though adoption were a dreadful, never-to-be-revealed revelation, and if Nik had been raised with that same kind of attitude—which he clearly had been—then it would be an extremely sensitive subject which he was not accustomed to talking about.

He was silent for several long minutes, his handsome dark head slightly bent, his eyes hooded. He was very disturbed by what she had told him and several times she thought he was about to speak but then his lips would compress again as though he didn't trust himself to do so. Leah would have loved him to share his thoughts but she quelled her urge to probe. It wasn't the time. But he still looked so shaken that she couldn't stop herself rising and crossing the room and closing her arms around him.

Briefly he went rigid in surprise.

'Forget about it,' she urged, dimly astonished by her own daring and the strong current of protectiveness which had propelled her to him. 'It's so unimport-ant——'

He startled her by laughing and placing his hands on her slim hips to haul her into the hard heat of his lithe frame. 'If you say so.'

She wondered how many hugs he had got growing up with that set of frozenly repressed individuals down-stairs. Maybe it had been her own presence which had soured almost everyone's response. But in the back of her mind Leah suspected something far nastier.

Did his sisters and their families resent Nik's power and success because they did not consider him to be a true Andreakis? Was that because Nik had been adopted by his parents so late in life? His siblings had already been adults and the adoption could well have come as an unpleasant shock, she reasoned. Yet that was so hatefully unfair when Nik was so generous towards them all and willing to go to such lengths to protect them!

And which one of them ... which one of that unlovely bunch *was* Nik protecting? Suddenly, Leah burned to know that secret, in defence of which Nik had sacrificed his own freedom. Now that his family had been person-

alised, she was eaten by her own curiosity, a raw need
to know who in Nik's eyes was worth that level of
protection.

'You look as though you're a thousand miles away.'

Drawn from her introspection, she met his dark eyes
and faint pink highlighted her cheeks.

'And I want you here,' he completed softly.

Her heartbeat shifted up in tempo, her mouth running
dry on the brink of a sudden quivering surge of intense
awareness. Instinct made her move against him with the
sinuousness of a cat seeking a caress and she heard the
catch of his breath in response a moment before he devoured her mouth with the hot, hard heat of his own.

His passion caught her unawares but the irresistible
force of desire washed over her, leaving her pliant in his
strong hold. On every level her body recognised him,
reached out to him with a need she could not control.
Her jacket fell to the carpet as he stripped it from her.
Fingers brushed against her spine and deftly released the
fastening on her bra and his hand closed around the
pouting swell of one breast, making her breath sob in
her throat.

He pressed her back on the bed and let his mouth
travel between her urgently sensitive nipples. The fire
consumed her, heat pooling in his loins, every centi-
metre of her slim form trembling with the hunger he had
unleashed on her. She looked up at him through passion-
glazed eyes as he stood over her, removing his own
clothing with hard, impatient hands, his glittering dark
gaze pinned to her with primal purpose.

And she sensed the wildness in him, read it in the stark
lines of his taut features, the slashing curve of his lips.
He couldn't take his eyes off her and she felt wanton
lying there with her breasts bare and her skirt rucked up
round her hips, the slender length of her thighs exposed.
But the excitement emanating from him kept her still,
powerless to fight the most basic of all human drives.

'This moment was all I could think of while I was making polite conversation and drinking coffee,' he revealed, staring down at her with unwavering intensity, hunger blatantly stamped in his strong face. 'I couldn't concentrate. Now the feeling surpasses even the anticipation.'

She looked up at him, her breasts rising and falling with the rapidity of her breathing. Naked, he was magnificent, a masculine symphony of sleek bone and muscle and golden skin. A flush of quivering heat enclosed her as he bent to unzip her skirt, slide it off, and she lay there submissive, pliant in a honeyed languor, but with every sense at fever pitch.

His tongue dipped into the shallow indentation of her navel. Her eyes shut, she reached out blindly for him, desperate for the physical contact she craved. He came to her and her mouth found his, her heart hammering madly inside her ribcage as her hands closed over the bunched muscles in his shoulders. His skin was hot, slightly damp, and he rolled over, taking her with him, one strong hand dispensing with the last barrier of clothing that separated her from him.

'Yes,' she moaned, arching her back in sudden delicious torment as he skimmed his knuckles down over her taut stomach and then spread his hand, holding her where she most needed to be touched but denying what every skin cell longed for.

'I don't know where to begin,' he muttered thickly against her swollen mouth, and she could feel him, hard and hotly aroused against her thigh. 'I want ... I want everything you have to give.'

Dazed sapphire eyes met incandescent jet and an almost terrifying excitement imprisoned her. He said something rough in Greek and pressed her back, plundered her mouth with his tongue and then drove her wild with every burning caress until there was nothing—no thought, no feeling beyond an overpowering, shattering need for more.

'*Now*,' he said, lifting from her, pressing back her thighs and filling her with one, hard thrust.

The intensity of her pleasure was mind-blowing. 'I need you...' she sobbed, at the peak of a wave of ecstasy more intense than anything she had ever experienced, and from that point on she was lost in a world of sensation that clawed everyday reality aside, leaving only the surging demands of her own body beneath his in control.

'Time to wake, *pethi mou*.'

She swam up through the lightening barriers of sleep and smiled contentedly. Nik's mouth brushed against hers but when she reached for him he wasn't there. She opened her eyes. He was standing by the bed, his hair still wet from the shower. He gave her a dazzling smile. 'Dinner is in one hour,' he delivered.

No way could she summon up a sense of urgency even though she knew she needed to wash her hair. She was lost in memories of the afternoon and the intimacy of watching Nik dress absorbed her as much as a brilliant and enthralling soap opera. Her cheeks warmed as memory served up the length of time they had spent in bed, the new skills she had been expertly taught, the amount of practice she had put in and the sheer exquisite pleasure of learning that Nik could be as helpless in the grip of passion as she was.

'Dress formal,' he told her, sliding his arms into a white silk shirt. 'I believe there is to be dancing. Since my mother is not a fan of the pastime, I can only assume she is pulling out all the stops to impress the Kiriakos clan.'

Leah sat up, pushing a hand through her wildly tousled hair, watching him with a wealth of tenderness in her still sleepy eyes. 'Why would she do that?'

Nik laughed wryly. 'Our families stopped socialising together when the engagement was broken off. There has been a definite coolness ever since.' He shrugged with fluid grace and then his mouth tightened. 'However, I cannot say that I admire the timing. Good manners should have dictated that this be a family evening alone.'

Leah knew what he was getting at but couldn't have cared less. When Evanthia Andreakis chose to entertain Nik's former fiancée and family the same day that she finally got to meet Nik's wife it was undoubtedly not a coincidence. It was a snub, as much of a snub as Leah had been dealt when her mother-in-law had barely acknowledged her existence earlier, but for Nik's sake she was prepared to dismiss such behaviour as being supremely beneath her notice. If anything she sympathised with Nik for having a mother still bent on signifying her disapproval five years after the event.

'If my mother were a younger woman I would have told her how I felt about her conduct towards you this afternoon,' Nik breathed grimly.

'Please don't get into any arguments over me.' But she was pleased that he had noticed, pleased that he was annoyed on her behalf.

'I would not have believed her capable of such foolishness. What does she hope to achieve? If you are not accorded respect, I will not visit this house again,' he intoned very quietly.

Leah was dismayed by the hard, unyielding edge to his level assurance. She knew he meant it. 'I don't want you to do that.'

'To be frank, I come here only out of duty. I hate this house and I despise most of the people currently staying in it. It is as though a cloud lifts when I walk out of it again.'

She was shocked by his ruthless candour. He was lowering his guard for the first time with her, the emotional distance he usually observed abruptly cast aside. Paradoxically, it shook her that Nik could hide so much from her. Earlier she had not even realised that he had either noticed or been angered by his family's reception of her. Now she could see that he was quietly seething about it, letting her know that the fur would fly if it continued. But that was the last thing she wanted.

'Nik...let them get used to me,' she heard herself urge tautly. 'Ponia made me laugh earlier because she said that all of them were hoping you'd dump me and get back with Eleni, and because your mother is obviously fond of her and they've never met me before I'm the one who must seem the intruder.'

Nik viewed her with narrowed eyes and a curled lip. 'Eleni is a happily married woman...even *my* family could not cling to hope in the face of that fact!' he derided with impatience.

He didn't know. He didn't know that Eleni's marriage had broken up.

'According to your niece, Eleni and her husband have split up,' Leah murmured.

Nik froze in the act of tying his bow-tie, an arrested expression stilling his features. He spun around. 'Since when?' he demanded.

A curious chill ran over Leah. 'I don't know...I don't know anything about it.'

'Ariadne should put a padlock on Ponia's tongue. Right now she's running around like a grenade with the pin pulled out!' Nik said curtly, his dark eyes hooded as he swung back to the mirror again.

And then there was nothing but silence. Nik might as well have been in a room on his own. Leah slid jerkily out of bed and vanished into the *en suite*. She had dropped a bombshell, that was obvious. Nik had been astonished at the news and then his whole face had closed as he'd mulled it over. So what did it mean to him? What did the idea that Eleni might be free and available mean to Nik? Anything...nothing? Maybe he was simply irritated that Eleni had not chosen to tell him the news personally.

Don't get carried away with your imagination, she scolded herself now. But she remembered the way Eleni had switched on like a neon light when she'd seen Nik, her beautiful face shedding all that natural cool and reserve. And that was not an image Leah was particularly happy to recall...

Naturally Nik hadn't waited to escort her downstairs. Leah entered the crowded salon, luminously lovely in an azure shoulderless evening gown which matched her eyes. And the first thing she saw was Nik and Eleni seated together in a far corner in deep conversation. So he's catching up on what he didn't know, she told herself, only it was a little difficult to believe that Eleni's radiant smile was accompanying the sad and stressful tale of a failed marriage. But Nik looked deadly serious, serious enough for both of them.

Ponia gave her a vague wave but appeared to be welded to the spot in front of the very handsome young man talking to her. Nik focused on her and instantly rose to his feet. By the time he had joined her, dinner had been announced.

'You cut in fine,' he said with a constrained smile, and it was that constraint where there had been none before that leapt out at her, like a chill wind unexpectedly spoiling a sunny day. 'But you look ravishing.'

You're a jealous, possessive, insecure idiot, a voice shrieked inside her head. But she could not resist the temptation to ask, 'Has Eleni's marriage broken up?'

Nik's gaze veiled. 'Yes.'

And that was it. Confirmation, no further discussion. Nor was a large, formal dinner party the background for a private conversation. To her surprise, Leah found herself seated to the immediate right of her hostess, with Nik directly opposite and Eleni several seats further down. Mrs Andreakis even made several frozen attempts at conversation in perfect English and Leah responded with the generosity of her nature but underneath she was thinking in some discomfiture, My goodness, Nik's been busy. Lines of strain marked his mother's face and she looked her age, something she had not looked earlier in the day.

It was a relief to be released from the dinner-table. Leah had eaten little. Ponia collared her as soon as she rose from her seat. 'I want you to meet somebody.'

The very handsome young man was yanked forward. His name was Dion. Wasn't he cute? Dion flushed and bristled but when he looked at Ponia Leah could see that he was helplessly hooked if not yet quite accustomed to the sensation of being shown off like a prize poodle.

'We're going to get engaged next year,' Ponia announced in a stage whisper.

So young, so sure, Leah reflected, feeling a hundred years old as she recalled just how she had felt about Nik at the same age. And five years on she was in even deeper. So who was to say that Ponia was too young to know her own mind?

'She told me at fourteen that she was going to marry him,' Nik sighed from behind her as the happy couple moved away, Ponia dragging Dion in her breathless wake. 'She even told me why.'

'Why?' Leah smiled.

'She wanted to see him smile...and he does, continually around her. He's twenty-two, coming to the end of his business course at Harvard and as serious as she's flighty. He's absolutely terrified she might find him boring by next year.'

'Do you think she will?' The music was playing in the ballroom and Dion and Ponia were already circling round the floor.

'No.' Nik gave a rueful laugh. 'I think she had the guts to follow her own heart and she didn't let pride come between them either when his family made it clear they didn't care for the connection. For that strength and that clarity I believe I even envy her.'

Leah shot him a veiled glance, catching the undertone of bitterness in his dark drawl, seeing it matched by a flash of stark regret in his clear gaze. Was he thinking about Eleni? Was he looking back and regretting the arrogance which had made him decide that Eleni was not for him all those years ago? And had Eleni let him go freely or with a brave smile that concealed her heartache? Watching her with Nik, Leah found it hard to believe that Eleni regarded him solely as a close friend.

Nik danced with her. He was a marvellous dancer but Leah was in an edgy mood, unable to relax, more prone to thinking unfortunate thoughts that harked back to the past she had sworn to bury. She rested her cheek on his shoulder and the familiar scent of him filled her with pain. Losing him . . . the idea of losing him terrified her. The knowledge that she couldn't lose him unless that certificate turned up was no consolation. All that did was remind her that Nik was not with her by choice.

She was introduced to Eleni's parents. They were polite and pleasant but she sensed the coolness underneath, knew that they were thinking that she was the woman who had stolen their daughter's fiancé from her five years ago. After a little while she excused herself and she was heading for the terrace and some fresh air when Stavros fell into step beside her.

'I haven't seen Ariadne tonight,' she remarked.

'Sadly, my wife didn't feel up to the festivities. She's resting,' he sighed.

'Is she ill?' Leah asked gently.

'Sick with nerves. She only suffers that here with her loving family,' he said, his mouth flattening with un-hidden contempt as he closed his hands tautly over the wrought-iron rail which girded the terrace from the gardens. He swivelled round and looked searchingly at Leah. 'Nik treating her like the plague doesn't help.'

Leah went pink, unprepared for that bluntness. 'I'm sorry... I——'

'I watched you together. You and Nik. You're close. I promised Ariadne faithfully that I would never speak to Nik, never approach him on this subject, but I gave no promise about you,' Stavros said with grim emphasis, each word carefully measured. 'So now I will talk to you and hope you have the heart to act as an intermediary.'

'An intermediary?' Leah frowned at him.

'Between us and Nik. Nik knows... I could tell you the very month and the year he changed towards my wife. I wanted to speak to him then. I wanted to know what he knew, what nonsense he had been told which could turn him against her to such an extent. But Ariadne almost had a nervous breakdown over the idea and I was silenced... but much against my will!'

Leah stared at him uncomfortably. 'Stavros... I don't know what you're talking about.'

'Not *you* too.' The older man sighed with immense weariness. 'Of course you know. Nik had only found out when you were newly married. He could not have kept that to himself. Thirty years ago Ariadne gave him up, but in her heart she *never* gave him up and she truly believed that she was doing what was best for him...'

Comprehension hit Leah in a sudden wave, leaving her dizzy and reeling with shock. Ariadne was not Nik's sister but Nik's mother, her child given up to her parents to raise as their own within her sight but not within her care. And Nik *knew*... Nik did know, and the last piece of the puzzle fell into place. Was this the family skeleton that her wretched father had threatened to drag out into the light of day? That Ariadne was not Nik's sister but in fact the woman who had brought him into the world?

'I want to be sure that Nik knows the truth,' Stavros asserted, too emotionally charged up now to take note of her reaction. 'All of the truth, not merely whatever his grandmother chose to tell him. Nik was never adopted. A birth certificate was falsified to enable Evanthia and Alexos to pretend that he was their child but though they went to great lengths they could not hope to fool Ariadne's sisters and the adoption story was coined for their benefit. Alexos wanted a son and he prevailed over his wife's wishes and insisted that they keep Nik, a child whom he could raise as his own but who was at least half an Andreakis.'

'You know the whole story——'

'Had I known it thirty years ago I would never have allowed them to do it!' Stavros asserted with unhidden anger. 'We were young. We did wrong. But they should have let us marry when they realised she was carrying our child. For that I can never forgive them!'

'You're Nik's father,' Leah whispered unevenly, staring at him with huge eyes.

Stavros frowned at her. 'You did not know that? And if you do not know it, are you telling me that Nik does not know it either?'

'It's not something we've talked about,' Leah said weakly, leaning back against the rail for support.

Stavros looked grimmer than ever. 'Maybe he does not want to know, maybe he blames us for his rotten childhood—and he has cause,' he conceded grudgingly.

'Do you think you could start at the beginning?' Leah suggested quietly.

Stavros was brief and succinct. He had been a student when he'd fallen in love with Ariadne Andreakis. He had neither the money nor the background to impress her parents then and the relationship had been broken up. Ariadne had not had the courage to fight her family. When her pregnancy was discovered, she had gone abroad with her mother. Stavros had not been told, had not even been aware of Nik's existence until he met up with Ariadne again a decade later.

'It almost killed me to learn what she had gone through alone. And to know I had a son I could not claim. But this time I would not be parted from Ariadne. I wore her down. I *made* her marry me in the teeth of their opposition!' he admitted with a satisfaction that strongly reminded her of Nik. 'Alexos was outraged and Evanthia hated the sight of me—and still does—but what could they do once the deed was done but put a face on it? Appearances count a lot to this family.'

'And then?'

'Then happiness was tempered with misery,' Stavros revealed bluntly. 'Ariadne believed we should be grateful that our son was within our sight. If he had been given away for adoption we might never have found him, never have known him...but ultimately I sometimes think that might have been less painful. Evanthia didn't love him, didn't treat him like a son, and the rest of the family resented him, this adopted child brought in to inherit over their heads.'

'And they still resent him,' Leah murmured feelingly.

'Yet he has multiplied their wealth a hundredfold. Alexos...he was a good man at heart,' Stavros conceded. 'He cared about Nik but he thought Ariadne was a weakling, so he was very tough on her son. But Ariadne is not weak. She coped with the situation until Nik began to avoid her and we realised that he knew.'

'About five years ago, I believe you said,' Leah framed unsteadily.

'It must have been a terrible shock but we had waited for so long, hoping that he might ask or find out or suspect,' Stavros muttered with a raw candour that brought tears to Leah's eyes. 'It wasn't our place to tell him if he had no suspicion. Ariadne promised her parents that she would never tell him. That was the price she paid. But that Nik should learn the truth of his parentage and then freeze her out... Neither one of us, in our innocence, expected that!'

Leah bowed her head, wondering what Nik did feel, struggling to make sense of behaviour that no longer made sense to her. Who did he think he was protecting? Ariadne or his grandmother or both of them?

'For her peace of mind, this *must* be resolved.' Stavros reached for her hand and squeezed it. 'So I ask you to raise this subject with Nik and discover if he knows the whole truth since it is very obvious that he will never approach us.'

'Yes.'

'She loves him very much; she makes excuses for him, blames herself but he is a grown man, a highly intelligent man,' Stavros said in a rough undertone. 'Why continue to accept me and not her? He makes no attempt to conceal his attachment to our daughter. Were I not bound by my promise to his mother I would have challenged him without fear.'

Leah lifted drowning eyes. 'I don't think Nik knows you're his father.'

The older man looked unconvinced and then noted the lines of stress on her delicate face. 'It is very selfish of me to drag you into this mess.'

'No.' She almost told him that she had been a part of that same mess longer than he could have possibly guessed. Had Max got his hands on Nik's original birth certificate? Was there any mention of who his father was? But it was beyond the bounds of belief that Nik had discovered his mother's identity without demanding further answers from *somebody*! The trail could only lead back to Evanthia Andreakis.

She took a deep breath. 'I'll talk to him when we get back to London... not here,' she stressed.

'Whatever the outcome, I will be in your debt.'

As Stavros moved away from her, Leah felt the weight of that burden. It wasn't a case of no news was good news. Nik was as volatile and unpredictable as Pandora's box and Stavros could have no idea just how

far Nik had been prepared to go to conceal the truth of
his parentage. It *had* to be that which Max had discovered—a birth certificate, capable of blowing the
Andreakis family sky-high even thirty years on. There
couldn't possibly be two such dangerous secrets in one
family...surely?

Nik was watching her across the width of the room.
She wondered if he was aware that she had just a very
long and private conversation with Stavros. The weight
of that guilty knowledge engulfed her, leaving her pale,
her facial bones stiff. She was tempted to rush in and
tell all, knew that it would be madness in such sur-
roundings. But even as she looked back at him Nik was
turning aside, his strong features coldly cast until Eleni,
standing several feet away, said something that made him
smile.

And though a few minutes later he joined her and she
spent what remained of the evening never far from him
she registered with a sinking heart that he had distanced
himself from her. The warmth had gone, to be replaced
by cool, polite constraint. And she felt cold inside and
afraid. The barriers he had smashed down in Paris weeks
ago had suddenly been replaced for no good reason that
she could see.

The change had come not from her but from him.
Maybe Eleni's presence reminded him of the terms of
his marriage...the life sentence he had once flung in
Leah's teeth. There was no free choice in a life sentence.
And suddenly Leah knew that for her there would be
no happiness until she could give Nik that choice...

CHAPTER TEN

NIK parted from her the instant they entered the London house. He had a lot of work to catch up on, he said. He would be leaving again as soon as he had changed.

'Don't hurry back on my account,' Leah urged with an acidity that was in direct proportion to the pain she was ramming down inside her.

He swung back, shooting her a grim glance. 'We'll talk when I get back.'

Why was she receiving the impression that she was the one at fault? She had done nothing. But since last night she had felt like Nik's gaoler. How would he react when she told him about her conversation with Stavros? Would she be telling him anything he didn't already know? How would he react when he realised that she now knew that secret? He had not trusted her enough to tell her himself. That fact bit deepest of all.

She walked into the drawing-room and her mouth twisted as she looked at her mother's writing bureau. 'Take an axe to it if you like!' Nik had derided. When she pulled down the flap that functioned as a writing surface she saw nothing new. The drawers and pigeon-holes were empty. She didn't use the bureau because it didn't lock. The key decoratively attached by a too short golden chain to the flap would not reach the keyhole. Such a foolish oversight on the part of the craftsman who had restored the piece.

It was only when she looked at that key now that she realised it bore a very close resemblance to the same key she had held in her hand inside that Paris bank. She broke the chain, hurting her hand in the process. The key had been lightly gilded to match the chain but the numbers engraved on it could still be read. It didn't even fit the lock on the flap. It was the key to another safety-deposit box. For five long years Nik had had his passport to freedom right under his own roof. Max would have enjoyed that irony.

She went to Nik's wing of the house. Her feet carried her up there, made that left turn on the landing of their own accord. He was pulling on a fresh shirt in the bedroom, so preoccupied with his own thoughts that he didn't even notice her entrance.

'Nik . . .' Her voice emerged hoarsely.

He spun fluidly round to face her, a winged ebony brow quirking as he saw her standing there, sapphire eyes glittering like jewels, the only flash of life in the still beauty of her face.

For a split-second she wanted to curl her fingers around the key and hide it. It had never occurred to her that it might take courage to hand it over, an even greater courage to face the likely consequences. But that awareness hit her now and, shamed by that momentary hesitation, she lifted her hand and dropped the key down on to the bed.

'Not a life sentence after all,' she heard herself say flatly.

There was not a flicker of comprehension in Nik's questioning scrutiny. He had never been so slow on the uptake. He stared at her and then back at the key blankly.

'It's the key to another safety-deposit box. Presumably it contains what you're after.' And she explained about the bureau.

'Cristo!' Nik whispered, coming back to life and sweeping up the key. 'All this time. I cannot believe it!'

Leah wandered over to the window. The key to the promised land of freedom. Either the end or the beginning of their marriage. Only time would tell her which for if Nik didn't want to let her go he wouldn't. On that level he was basic.

'There's something else we have to discuss.'

'Can it not wait?' he demanded with impatience. 'I won't be able to rest until I fly back to Paris and try out this key.'

'No, I'm afraid this can't. You see, I happen to know what is in that box. Your birth certificate.' Leah turned her head.

His starkly handsome features were fiercely clenched. 'And where did you come by that information?'

Leah loosed a jagged laugh. 'Well, certainly not from you. Stavros chose to confide in me——'

'*Stavros*?' Nik ejaculated incredulously.

'He asked me to act as an intermediary. He assumed that I was in your confidence,' Leah revealed. 'So I now know that Ariadne is your natural mother.'

'Stavros is aware of this?' Nik was ashen, his dark gaze nailed to her.

'Look, it's none of my business,' Leah breathed because Nik, with his silence, had made it so crushingly clear that it wasn't.

'For how long has he known?' he launched at her rawly.

Her brow furrowed. He really didn't know. He really didn't know that Stavros was his father and she did not want to be the one to tell him.

'*Theos mou* . . . if he knew, there was no need for me to worry that it might destroy their marriage!' he vented in sudden savage frustration.

And with those few words Nik told her so much. He did not know who his father was. He had assumed he was a dark secret in Ariadne's past, the kind of secret a conservative Greek husband would not be able to swallow. So Nik had been protecting Ariadne. And he was none too pleased to discover that his sacrifice had been in vain.

'Stavros knows everything about your parentage. He wants to talk to you. He's worried about the effect this continuing secrecy is having on Ariadne.'

Nik muttered something in Greek, both hands clenching. 'Then why did he not approach me personally?'

'He promised her that he would never do that, just as she promised your grandparents that she would never tell you.'

'She is ashamed of me.'

'I don't think so, and if you weren't so stubborn and so damnably proud you might have found that out for yourself by now!' Leah shot at him shakily.

Nik dealt her a look of such fury that she was pinned to the spot. 'The first time I saw her after I found out I did attempt to speak to her. She burst into tears and ran away!' he derided. 'She was hysterical and terrified.'

And that had been it for Nik. He must have felt absolutely betrayed by the deception which had been practised on him for over twenty years. He would have appeared angry and bitter and accusing, not hurt. He wouldn't have shown the hurt. Unprepared to deal with his sudden knowledge, Ariadne had panicked and burnt her boats simultaneously.

With an abruptness that startled her, Nik turned away. 'So what else do we have to discuss? Our marriage?' he murmured without any emotion at all. 'That is very simple. You stay or you go. Try to make your mind up before I return from Paris.'

Leah stood there in stunned silence. Shattered, she watched him shrug his broad shoulders gracefully into his jacket. There was a whirring sound in her eardrums. The silence closed in around her. Never in her life had she imagined such humiliation. She walked out of the room, her stomach clenched tight with nausea, her breath rasping in her aching throat.

If he had uncorked the champagne and danced it would have been civilised in comparison with that casual, unemotional statement of total indifference. His cruelty astounded her. But then Nik didn't have any reason to pretend any more. He was free and he could not have told her more candidly that he wanted his freedom. He might just as well have said, There's the door... use it! It was over... just like that. She was surplus to requirements.

And yet yesterday... Yesterday, she appreciated numbly, was a million miles removed from today when she had given him that key. That day in the bank vault Nik had said that Max had known he would dump her like a hot potato if he ever got his hands on that certificate. In anger, he had been honest, but only that once. As long as the pressure was on, he had been determined to keep their marriage intact by whatever means were within his power. And, being Nik, conscience hadn't got a look-in!

And yet yesterday... Dear God! As the erotic imagery of what she had naïvely assumed to be their mutual passion bombarded her she covered her face, torn apart by the pain which was threatening to swallow her alive. How could you be that intimate with another human being and not care in the slightest about that person's feelings? But then she knew how and why, didn't she?

Nik was the man who had told her that love had terrified him, Nik, who impressed one as being utterly without fear. He had grown up without love and had learnt to do without it. When even the security of what he had believed to be his background had been torn from him by her father when he was twenty-five he had been further hardened, and if he was bitter about his family he had every right to be. He had bottled it all up and brooded about it. That was Nik: keep it all to himself, share nothing, betray no response lest he make himself

vulnerable and risk an ounce of the ferocious pride which
powered him.

It was a pity he hadn't thought of her pride . . . but
then what would have been the point? The charade Max
had begun had been played out to its final act. And Nik
wanted his life back—*now*. Not another hour, not
another day.

She shuddered, chilled to the marrow by his cruelty.
Now the freedom she had fought for mere weeks ago
had been handed to her on a plate. Nik would not wait
to be free of Max's daughter. Well, damn him to hell,
she thought as she wiped at her overflowing eyes. He
was a complete bastard and he was really doing her a
favour. No woman worthy of her sex would droop
around weeping wetly over a creep like Nik Andreakis!

'That was really something, honey. It took me way back.'
As Leah's fingers lifted from the keyboard the handsome
American leaning up against the piano treated her to a
look of unvarnished admiration. 'Would you happen to
know . . . ?' He whistled a couple of out-of-tune bars and
she laughed and obliged. As he returned with noticeable
reluctance to his seat she smiled.

At this hour the dimly lit lounge was usually busier
and she got few personal requests. Then she played what
she wanted, perfectly aware that she was just supplying
a little background mood music to add to the relaxed
atmosphere that the hotel management liked to extend
to their wealthy clientele. She wasn't very well paid but
she was coping and she had a couple of interviews for
other jobs set up for the following week.

In short, she was surviving. It had been a month since
she had walked out of Nik's life. She had learnt the virtue
of keeping constantly busy. And she was so darned tired
that she slept like a log at night when she finally fell
into bed.

She planned the daylight hours like a military combatant. She had signed up for a computer course. She scanned the employment columns, wrote off for any jobs that might be within her reach and plenty that probably weren't. And every morning she rose with the prayer that *this* would be the day she didn't think of Nik once! Unhappily, however, playing the piano wasn't a good defence against him. He would drift into her mind and hover with amazing persistence until she booted him out again.

So when Leah glanced up from the keyboard and saw Nik standing mere feet away she didn't initially register that he was *real*. It was as though her memory had served him up. Her hands kept on playing but her sapphire eyes were nailed to the quite dazzling manifestation of her darkest desires. For that was what he was. He belonged in a locked drawer labelled 'Unhealthy Obsession'.

'Play for me,' he drawled softly.

Her fingers had stilled without her even realising it. Her heart jumped into her throat. He cast a long shadow. She dropped her eyes, rigid with angry vulnerability. Why and how had he tracked her down?

'Please...' he murmured, and if the word sounded a little strange on his lips it was probably because it was unfamiliar to him.

'What would you like me to play?' she enquired as if he were a customer but without the polite smile.

'Anything.'

'You can't name a single composer, can you?' she derided.

'Chopin.' He meant business. The total philistine had come prepared.

She gave him Beethoven, was well aware that he wouldn't know the difference and then felt rather mean and contemptible. He stayed by the piano throughout, which infuriated her. All she could see of him was his

shadow and the lean fingers of one shapely hand and
that was more than enough to unsettle her.

'What do you want?' she muttered tightly, seeing the
manager watching them from the bar, conscious that she
had never been more appreciative of the blanket ban on
her fraternising with guests or casual customers.

'The barman told me you have a break at nine.'

'Not to share with you.'

Nik laid a worn leather jewel-box down on top of the
piano. 'Your mother's necklace.'

'I sold it!'

'I'm giving it back to you.'

'I don't want it!' she spat. 'And I want you to go
away and leave me alone!'

'Is this gentleman a friend of yours, Miss Harrington?'

Leah spun round. The assistant manager who had been
watching them from the bar had decided to join the fray.

'No,' she said.

'If I were you I would ignore that little white lie,' Nik
advised with a sardonic smile. 'Your pianist is my wife.'

'Is that true?'

She wanted to scream that it was a dirty, devious mis-
representation of the true facts. But she had a hideous
premonition that Nik would be more than equal to continuing the dispute. Seething, she gave a jerky nod.

'And she's about to take her break,' Nik added so
smoothly that she wanted to hit him.

She crossed the lounge to the table reserved for her
use near the bar. Nik settled down opposite and stared
at her, just stared, not a single expression crossing his
startlingly handsome features. He had lost weight, she
noted, enough to accentuate the angle of his cheekbones
and the hard line of his jaw. Her mother's jewel-box,
which she had ignored and he had picked up, now sat
on the table between them.

'How did you find me?' she snapped.

'With effort.'

'What do you want?'

'I wanted you to see this.' Calmly, from an inside pocket he withdrew a slip of paper, unfolded it and placed it between them. 'You have that right, don't you think?'

The certificate. She didn't know whether to laugh or cry. The certification that proved that a Nikos Andreakis had been born to an Ariadne Andreakis in a Swiss clinic thirty years ago.

'There is no entry under father. When I challenged Evanthia I was told that he was a married man, whom my mother had refused to name. I was also warned that Stavros had no idea that his wife had ever given birth to an illegitimate child. I was reminded of all the advantages the deception had gained me, the life I might have led had I not been fortunate enough to be kept in the family. I was also told that it was my duty to keep quiet and never to shame Ariadne with the reminder of our true relationship.' Nik completed with perceptible harshness.

Involuntarily, Leah gave him a look of distress. 'That was so cruel.'

'Until the day Max produced this I had no idea that I was not Evanthia's child. I was devastated by the extent of their deceit. All those years nobody had breathed a word. I turned on Ariadne. I wanted answers. I was entitled to them. But she ran,' he reminded her. 'And when she did that she confirmed everything that Evanthia had told me. So I did not approach her again. She was so nervous, I was afraid she would betray us all.'

'You cared about her.' She said it for him because she knew how hard he would find saying it.

'Of course,' he said gruffly, retrieving the certificate.

'Have you spoken to her now?'

'Yes. And Stavros.' Nik sent her a sudden shimmering glance. 'Thank you so much for warning me.'

She flushed. 'I didn't think you'd want me breaking the news.'

'I'm delighted with Stavros. All my life I have dreamt of having a father who threatened to knock my teeth down my throat if I upset my mother!'

Leah gazed at him in dismay.

'So now I know where I get my temper from.' He gave her a rather rueful smile that yanked painfully at her heartstrings. 'I like him. I always liked him. He's a maverick like me. And some day, when Evanthia can no longer feel threatened by the truth,' he phrased carefully, 'we will own each other publicly and not give a damn.'

'Wonderful. I'm glad it's all sorted out,' Leah murmured, not sounding as if she was glad at all because she finally understood why he had come to see her. He thought he owed her the happy ending to the story which Max had started with a nightmare.

Silence fell, and not a comfortable one either. Nik glanced at his watch.

'Don't let me keep you.' Leah wondered if he could hear the cracking sound of her heart. She would rather not have seen him at all than see him sitting there, patently at a loss as to what to say next.

'I've bought a house in the country,' he said abruptly. 'I've put the London house on the market.'

A fresh start, another nail in her coffin. Valiantly she tried to see Nik in green wellies and failed. Living in the country had been her dream, not his.

'I thought maybe you'd... well, maybe you'd like to come and see it.'

'Why?' This was getting brutal, she thought in agony.

'It was just an idea.' He spread a brown hand, very nearly knocked his untouched drink over, and righted it with a stifled curse.

Silence fell again, alive with throbbing undertones of tension.

'You found yourself a job,' he began in what looked like near desperation.

'I won't always be here,' Leah told him tightly. 'It's a start. I'm getting by just fine, if that's what's bothering you.'

'Why should it?' He stared down broodingly into his drink.

'Maybe you'd have liked me to fall flat on my face!'

'Maybe.' He didn't deny it.

'Have you heard from my solicitor yet?' Misery made Leah masochistic.

The silence fell again like a thunderclap.

'You dumped all my socks,' Nik said grimly.

She went from pale to beetroot and refused to meet his eyes. 'It was a kind of statement.'

'I got the message.'

'It was childish,' she conceded painfully, running a finger round and round the rim of her glass. 'How's Eleni?' And then she couldn't believe she had asked him such a dead-give-away question.

'Happy... Her husband came crawling back the day of the dinner. She's promised to cut her working day down and he's promised to learn how to cook or some such bloody thing!' Nik dismissed, his curled lip emphasising his chauvinistic disbelief.

'Was that what you were talking about that night?' Leah prompted shakily, her every suspicion shot down in flames.

'Mostly she was telling me what a dinosaur I am.'

'Tell me more.'

'That I was one of life's takers, that I broke her heart five years ago and didn't notice,' he bit out shortly. 'And that if I had married her and done to her what I had done to you she would have personally castrated me.'

Eleni had taken revenge in the sweetest, most feminine way possible but she couldn't have done it had she not got over Nik. The silence was back, louder, tenser and more debilitating than ever. Leah's mouth ran dry. Something stronger than she was made her look up, and her blue eyes clashed with his black ones.

'Will you sleep with me tonight?'

If her lower lip hadn't been joined to her upper, it would have hit the floor with a crash. She just could not believe Nik had said that. But he looked back at her in unashamed challenge, every line of his taut features harshly delineated by the wall light behind him.

'I won't even dignify that proposition with an answer,' she managed shakily.

'Why not?'

'I just do not believe you are saying this to me——'

'Believe it,' he advised, running rampantly hungry black eyes over every inch of her visible above the table-top.

'I am in the process of divorcing you!'

'There hasn't been anyone else,' he asserted in a driven undertone as if he expected that to make all the difference. 'I haven't even looked at another woman. I don't even want another woman. I just want you!'

'Then you've got a problem.' Trembling like a leaf, Leah stood up, and all but drowned in the sexual charge of his glittering gaze. And she wanted him so much in spite of everything that she hated herself.

He caught her hand, preventing her from walking away. 'I shouldn't have asked . . . it wasn't what I meant to say,' he grated.

'But it was exactly what you were bloody well thinking about!' she shot down at him, and trailed her fingers free to walk back to the piano.

All he ever thought about, if anyone had cared to ask her. He still wanted her. It had taken him a month to appreciate the fact that sexually he had still to sate that inconvenient craving in her direction. So what did he do? She shivered with sheer rage. He just asked, 'Will you sleep with me tonight?' In Greece he had said 'you could make me beg'. And she would. She would make him crawl over broken glass and beg and she would still say no! But it wouldn't make her feel a whole lot better.

Out of the corner of her eye, she watched him spring up and stride out of the bar. And that didn't make her feel better either although it certainly should have done. She wanted to put her head down and sob her heart out but she had an audience of at least twenty people and a job to consider.

It was four in the morning before she slept. Her bed-sit felt claustrophobic. There was no room to pace. Her mattress had the consistency of rock. But she didn't cry; she was damned if she would cry over him.

Someone banged on the door at eight. And whoever it was was persistent. Leah dragged herself up, pulled on her wrap and opened it. A huge bunch of red roses was stuffed into her startled arms, Nik in their wake, devious as ever, taking advantage of her sleepy astonishment to walk in and shut the door behind him.

'And what do you expect me to do with these?' she rose above her disbelief to screech, murderously conscious of the make-up she hadn't bothered to take off the night before, the panda circles round her eyes, the hair standing on end and Nik poised there like an advert for Italian suits and perfect grooming.

'You put them in water,' he suggested doggedly.

Leah pushed unsteady fingers through her messy hair and just stared at him, her bewilderment writ large in her eyes. 'What is the matter with you?'

He studied her for several taut seconds and then swung away in silence. Leah took the opportunity to wash her face at the sink and drag a comb through her hair and was filled with self-loathing for herself as she did both.

'There was only a very small number of women I actually slept with during those years,' he volunteered stiffly. 'Most the first year, nobody at all the last.'

The dreaded tears lashed her prickling eyes in an acid surge. And how was she supposed to react to that startling piece of information?

But she didn't have to think. It just happened. She lifted those roses and hit him with them from behind. He turned, but instead of making an effort to defend himself he just stood there without even putting his hands up to protect his face as she battered him again. Several buds dropped on the worn carpet and the bouquet just dropped out of her suddenly nerveless hands. She felt like a maniac in the grip of a compulsive need to kill but the fact that he simply let her attack him defeated her.

Absolutely drained, she collapsed down on the foot of the bed and bowed her head, tears raining soundlessly down her cheeks. Nik crouched down in front of her and grabbed at her hands. 'Please come home,' he breathed roughly.

'I can't!'

'I won't ever ask what you've been doing this last month. I promise. I won't ever mention Woods again,' he swore feverishly. 'I can do it. I can stop being jealous. You think I can't but I can!'

Her tongue snaked out to moisten her lips. She opened wet eyes and focused on his downbent glossy head. 'You were jealous?'

'Devoured by it; what do you think I am—a stone?' he muttered savagely. 'When I saw those photos I was ripped apart. I couldn't handle them and I knew if I didn't I would lose you . . . and I have. But I've got over it now.'

'Nik . . .' Her throat had gone all tight.

'That night in Athens I could see you were thinking about him,' he said with dark emphasis. 'And I thought, How am I going to live with this?'

'I was thinking about you. Stavros had just dumped your parentage on me and I felt so guilty knowing what you didn't know,' she explained in a rush.

'I had no idea you had been talking to Stavros. And when you gave me that key the next day... the way you did it, your attitude... I knew the reward you expected was your freedom,' he murmured tautly. 'I couldn't force you to stay, not if you were in love with Woods. It would have been pointless. The decision had to be yours... and I really did not want to be around when you made it.'

It was an admission of cowardice which she had never expected to hear from Nik. She saw how her insecurity and her fear of putting her pride on the line had made her leap to conclusions and misinterpret his words. He had been the one who had pressured *her* into staying with their marriage. Once he had that key, he had believed that what happened next had to be her choice, her decision, for all along Leah had been the partner seeking a way out of their marriage.

She swallowed hard. 'I'm not in love with Paul——'

'Those photographs say different.' Releasing her hands, Nik sprang up and walked over to the window.

'Photos can be deceptive. I haven't even seen Paul since that time he came to the house and it was over then.' In a few words she explained why. 'It was just an infatuation, an adventure... whatever you want to call it. I was bored and lonely and I suppose I wanted what I had never had.'

'What you could have had with me had I not been too bitter and too proud to offer it.' Nik swung back to her, his strong features clenched hard. 'You have been more honest with me than I deserve, *pethi mou*. Had I lost you it would have been my own fault. I did fall in love with you the first time I saw you... you did not mistake my feelings. It was like being hit by lightning and when I got over the shock all I wanted to do was run——'

Arrested by what he was telling her, Leah tried and failed to swallow. 'But——?'

'But you might as well have tied my ankles together,' he muttered with raw self-derision, his mouth taking on a sardonic curve. 'I couldn't stay away. You were too young. I wasn't ready for marriage. But if I was not I knew that some other man might be...that if I walked away there was very little chance that you would be around when I chose to come back.'

'I can't believe you felt like that,' Leah whispered, afraid to believe in what he had denied for so long, afraid to believe that she had not, after all, been wrong about what she had sensed in Nik all those years ago, that that instant desperate attraction had indeed been mutual.

Lustrous dark eyes rested on her levelly. 'I did. But I didn't know how to handle it and I'm afraid I resented the hold you had on me. Then Max changed everything. He made my mind up for me. Suddenly I had no choice...'

Ashamed of what her father had done, she studied the carpet beneath her bare toes.

'Nobody had ever made me do anything I didn't want to do before. I couldn't believe that I could be that powerless,' he admitted harshly. 'I felt like some kind of stud stallion your father was buying for you! Trapped by a teenager. I was in a rage for months on end after it. And I swore to myself that you would get nothing that I did not choose to give out of our marriage!'

Thank you, Max, Leah thought bitterly. Thank you so much for smashing what we could have had together before it even got off the ground. She knew Nik well enough to know exactly how he had felt then. Caged, blackmailed, humiliated. She remembered the aura of silent menace that had surrounded him during the first year of their marriage but he had never once let any of it out, which said one hell of a lot for his self-control.

'I can understand that.'

'We had been married for a couple of years before I began to want you again.' Nik held her startled scrutiny with fierce determination. 'No, I didn't show it. I would have cut off my hands sooner than come near you!' he admitted. 'My pride revolted against the concept of surrendering further to Max's blackmail. You were the one woman in the world I wouldn't touch.'

That hurt so much but she should have seen it for herself. He had told her this before. 'Yes.'

'I didn't consider you. It was a fight between me and Max and you were the pawn in the middle. I didn't have to consider you. In the back of my mind you were there, in my house, my wife, I couldn't touch you but nobody else could either. And I could just about live with that.'

'I was on ice,' she said, with a jagged laugh.

'But by the time Max died I had already decided that you would stay as my wife and then, when the choosing was mine, it would become a real marriage. You know, it did not cross my mind that you would have any other ideas,' he confessed with a stark flush illuminating his hard cheekbones, a combination of discomfiture and shame in his clear gaze. 'You had accepted the situation for so long——'

'You thought you just had to say the word,' Leah filled in, her own skin pink but a certain amount of amusement tactfully concealed. He was an arrogant bastard but at least he was honest about his failings.

'I thought you loved me . . . that that was why you had stayed.'

'Faithful Penelope?'

'It was a very conceited assumption to make.'

But not an assumption made without encouragement, she realised.

'Hearing you on the phone to Woods was devastating, but perhaps no more than I had asked for,' he allowed tautly. 'But you wanted to leave me and I was forced to take extraordinary measures to keep you. I did not

seriously believe that there was any real danger of that
certificate still being a threat——'

'You didn't?' Leah prompted in astonishment, rising
to her feet.

'I just used it as a means of holding on to you and
forcing you to give our marriage a chance. And I had
no right to do that. Pride and resentment had stopped
me from taking that same chance while Max was alive.
But I could not face losing you.'

'Nobody else to buy you socks,' she said flippantly as
she moved restively about the confines of the cluttered
room.

'Until recently I had enough socks to do me a lifetime.'

Then a long, pulsing silence. Nik cleared his throat.
'When I said that I envied Ponia her strength in refusing
to give Dion Kiriakos up——'

'Dion is a Kiriakos?'

'Eleni's kid brother. Didn't you realise that?'

Leah shook her head, belatedly understanding why the
Kiriakos clan had been there in force that evening.

Nik cleared his throat again, sounding almost hesitant.
'Ponia didn't allow pride to come between her and her
heart. I did.'

Sapphire eyes flew to his taut features and all of a
sudden she knew what he was trying to say, what he was
having such a very hard struggle to say, and what he
probably would have avoided saying altogether if he
could have got away with 'Will you sleep with me
tonight?'

'You can write it down if it's easier,' she said unsteadily, happiness shrilling through her in an un-
stoppable wave. For once she was ahead of him.

'When I came back from Paris and you weren't there,
it was like coming back to a desert,' he breathed with a
ragged edge to his voice. 'I had gambled and I had lost.
You were out of there like you were escaping a prison
camp! I *need* you to come home.'

'You're selling it,' she reminded him with a spark of cruelty she had not known she possessed until that moment.

'It doesn't matter that you don't love me.' He looked at her in blatant desperation, both hands clasped tight with the height of his tension.

'The jury's still out on that one.'

'I love you very much,' he muttered between clenched teeth.

'And I love you too but I wasn't coming back until you said it.'

'At times like this maybe I should pine for the quiet, tractable woman you used to be!' He hauled her into his arms as he said it so she didn't take him seriously. It was heaven to be back there in his arms and for a long time there was silence and they just stood there locked together feverishly like the magnets Ponia had once accused them of being.

'I have missed you every hour of every day,' Nik swore, taking her mouth in a passionate assault that sent her every sense winging skywards, intense relief shuddering through his lean, hard body as he held her close. 'I thought I had lost you.'

A very long time later, when they had both surfaced from the physical expression of a mutually unhealthy obsession, Leah whispered softly, 'How did you feel when I dumped your socks?'

'If you hadn't been angry with me you wouldn't have taken the time to do it. That gave me hope,' he confided with a slumbrous smile.

'You were lucky I didn't slash your suits to bits!'

'That would have given me even more hope, but I do think I ought to mention that I have no desire to learn how to cook,' he murmured mockingly.

Leah ran a possessive hand over his hair-roughened chest. 'You have one or two other talents.'

Dark eyes scanned her suggestive smile. 'You think so?'

'Nik, I *know* so. Why waste time in the kitchen when you're so good in the boardroom?' she asked deadpan.

'You little witch,' he groaned, and kissed her again.

'I want to see that house you've bought,' she told him.

'I bought it for you.'

'Did you?'

He kissed her a third time and succeeded in distracting her.

It was late in the day before she got to tour that house where their new life together would begin, shorn of the past, shorn of everything but the simple fact that they loved each other.

HARLEQUIN  PRESENTS®

Don't be late for the wedding!

Be sure to make a date in your diary for the happy event—
The seventh in our tantalizing new selection of stories...

Wedlocked!

Bonded in matrimony, torn by desire...

To Have and To Hold by Sally Wentworth
Harlequin Presents #1787

"Gripping and enticing..."—*Romantic Times*

Marriage to Rhys might seem the answer to all Alix's
dreams...after all, she'd fallen in love with him at first sight.

But Rhys only proposed to Alix because she'd make him
the *perfect* wife.

Then Alix decided to take control of her own destiny, and Rhys
found that he couldn't live without her!

Available in January wherever Harlequin books are sold.

MILLION DOLLAR SWEEPSTAKES (III)

No purchase necessary. To enter, follow the directions published. Method of entry may vary. For eligibility, entries must be received no later than March 31, 1996. No liability is assumed for printing errors, lost, late or misdirected entries. Odds of winning are determined by the number of eligible entries distributed and received. Prizewinners will be determined no later than June 30, 1996.

Sweepstakes open to residents of the U.S. (except Puerto Rico), Canada, Europe and Taiwan who are 18 years of age or older. All applicable laws and regulations apply. Sweepstakes offer void wherever prohibited by law. Values of all prizes are in U.S. currency. This sweepstakes is presented by Torstar Corp., its subsidiaries and affiliates, in conjunction with book, merchandise and/or product offerings. For a copy of the Official Rules send a self-addressed, stamped envelope (WA residents need not affix return postage) to: MILLION DOLLAR SWEEPSTAKES (III) Rules, P.O. Box 4573, Blair, NE 68009, USA.

EXTRA BONUS PRIZE DRAWING

No purchase necessary. The Extra Bonus Prize will be awarded in a random drawing to be conducted no later than 5/30/96 from among all entries received. To qualify, entries must be received by 3/31/96 and comply with published directions. Drawing open to residents of the U.S. (except Puerto Rico), Canada, Europe and Taiwan who are 18 years of age or older. All applicable laws and regulations apply; offer void wherever prohibited by law. Odds of winning are dependent upon number of eligibile entries received. Prize is valued in U.S. currency. The offer is presented by Torstar Corp., its subsidiaries and affiliates in conjunction with book, merchandise and/or product offering. For a copy of the Official Rules governing this sweepstakes, send a self-addressed, stamped envelope (WA residents need not affix return postage) to: Extra Bonus Prize Drawing Rules, P.O. Box 4590, Blair, NE 68009, USA.

SWP-H1295

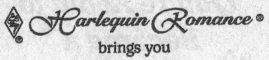 *Harlequin Romance* ®

brings you

How the West Was Wooed!

Harlequin Romance would like to welcome you
Back to the Ranch again in 1996 with our new
miniseries, Hitched! We've rounded up twelve of our
most popular authors, and the result is a whole year
of romance, Western-style. Every month we'll be
bringing you a spirited, independent woman whose
heart is about to be lassoed by a rugged, handsome,
one-hundred-percent cowboy!

Watch for books branded Hitched! in the coming
months. We'll be featuring all your favorite
writers including, **Patricia Knoll, Ruth Jean Dale,
Rebecca Winters** and **Patricia Wilson**, to mention
a few!

You're About to Become a *Privileged Woman*

Reap the rewards of fabulous free gifts and benefits with proofs-of-purchase from Harlequin and Silhouette books

Pages & Privileges™

It's our way of thanking you for buying our books at your favorite retail stores.

Harlequin and Silhouette— the most privileged readers in the world!

For more information about Harlequin and Silhouette's PAGES & PRIVILEGES program call the Pages & Privileges Benefits Desk: 1-503-794-2499

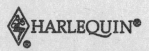

◈ HARLEQUIN®

HP-PP87